# Ancient Scottish Tales

Born on 4 August 1790 in Peterhead, Aberdeenshire, Peter Buchan was a Scottish collector of ballads and folktales, an editor and printer. In 1813, he married Margaret Mathew, with whom he would go on to have 10 children, and he was a jobbing tradesman when he went to Stirling in 1816 to learn the printing process before establishing his own business as a printer in Peterhead.

Through the 1830s and 40s, the family moved to Aberdeen, then south to Glasgow, before moving to a property near Dennyloanhead, Stirlingshire, and despite his various unsuccessful attempts to obtain employment in Edinburgh and London to supplement his literary career, Buchan devoted himself to collecting old Scottish songs and ballads from oral sources.

In 1825, he published *"Gleanings of Scotch, English, and Irish Scarce Old Ballads,"* and 3 years later, *"Ancient Ballads and Songs of the North of Scotland"*—a collection which contained a large number of ballads that had not been published at that time, as well as discovering new versions of existing ones. His work was known to contemporaries such as Charles Kirkpatrick Sharpe, William Motherwell, and Sir Walter Scott, who referred to Buchan's collection in the 1830, and final, edition of *"Minstrelsy of the Scottish Border,"* an anthology of Border ballads.

Buchan also compiled a collection of folk and fairytales, the original manuscript of which dates from 1827-9 and was known to John Francis Campbell, who discussed them in the Introduction to his *"Popular Tales of the West Highlands"* (1860), and Robert Chambers. In fact, the story of 'The Red Etin' included in the revised 1841 edition of Chambers' *"Popular Rhymes of Scotland,"* within the new section entitled *'Fireside Nursery Stories,'* is stated as being from Buchan's "curious manuscript collection." The Tales as a whole were published, with a limited print run and an introduction by John A. Fairley, in 1908, over 50 years after Buchan's death on a visit to London on 19 September 1854.

# ANCIENT SCOTTISH TALES

*Traditional, Romantic & Legendary Folk and Fairy Tales of the Highlands*

### PETER BUCHAN

#### UNABRIDGED EDITION
*Adapted by Rachel Louise Lawrence*

This unabridged adaption of *"Ancient Scottish Tales: An Unpublished Collection Made by Peter Buchan with an introduction by John A. Fairley"* (1908) first published in 2019 by Blackdown Publications

ISBN-13: 978-1671813830

Copyright © Rachel Louise Lawrence 2019

Illustration on cover by Walter Crane (1845-1915)

The rights of Rachel Louise Lawrence to be identified as the author of this work has been asserted by her in accordance with the Copyright, Designs and Patents Act 1988.

All rights reserved. No part of this publication may be reproduced, stored in or introduced into a retrieval system or transmitted, in any form, or by any means (electronic, mechanical, photocopying, recording or otherwise) without the prior permission of the author. Any person who does any unauthorised act in relation to this publication may be liable to criminal prosecution and civil claims for damages.

# Contents

| | | |
|---|---|---|
| I | *The Red Etin* | 1 |
| II | *The Young Prince* | 9 |
| III | *The History of Mr Greenwood* | 13 |
| IV | *The Cruel Stepmother* | 19 |
| V | *Rashen Coatie* | 26 |
| VI | *The Brown Bull of Ringlewood* | 32 |
| VII | *The Thriftless Wife* | 37 |
| VIII | *Green Sleeves* | 43 |
| IX | *The Prince with the White Petticoat* | 56 |
| X | *The Black Cat* | 61 |
| XI | *The Widow's Son and an Old Man* | 64 |
| XII | *The Widow's Son and the King's Daughter* | 67 |
| XIII | *The King of Morocco* | 73 |
| XIV | *The Princess of the Blue Mountains* | 77 |
| | Notes | 83 |

# Ancient Scottish Tales

Peter Buchan

## Buchan's Epigraph

"I take it to be a great advantage, that one can amuse one's self with an *old idle story* in these stormy times." *Lord Buchan*

# I
## *The Red Etin*

There once lived, near the burgh of Auchtermuchty in Fife, two poor widows who were unable to pay the rent of the small plot of ground allotted to them by the farmer whose sub-tenants they were.

This being the case, their landlord insisted on their sending away their sons to some employment, that they might be better able to pay their rents, as they were grown up, and able to something for themselves and their mothers.

These old women, though loath to part with their sons, having no alternative left to them, agreed that they must part. Having communicated their situation to each of the sons separately, these young men determined to seek their fortune in some distant country.

The first one, therefore, at the request of his mother, went to the well and fetched a jar of water, which was to be used to bake a loaf of bread for his journey; and however large or small the quantity of water he brought back with him, the size of the loaf was to be in proportion.

Having been furnished with a broken pitcher, however, the water had nearly all streamed out through the cracks before the lad got home, so that his loaf, in consequence, was very small. His mother then asked him, "Will you accept half of this bread with my blessing, or the whole of it with my curse?"

As he did not know how far he might need to travel, and as he did not know when or how he might get other provisions, he said, "I would prefer the whole loaf, come what may of your curse."

The consequence then was that, by slighting her blessing for the sake of a piece of bread, she prayed that her curse might attend him wherever he went, and blast him from top to toe. Under these unfavourable circumstances, he commenced his travels.

Being on friendly terms with his fellow young man, he gave him a knife, which was to be kept safe until his return, as it had the virtue of appearing bright and shiny when the owner was well, but if anything happened to him on his travels, it would immediately turn dim and rust. The second lad was to stay on for some time with his mother, and if the first succeeded well, he was then to pursue his journey.

The first young man, having wished farewell to his friends, departed. The first sight to secure his attention was a man herding a flock of sheep. He asked of this old shepherd, "To whom do these sheep belong?"

The old man answered,

> "The Red Etin of Ireland
>     Once lived in Bellygan,
> And stole King Malcolm's daughter,
>     The King of fair Scotland.
>
> He beats her, he binds her,
>     He lays her in a band;

> And every day he strikes her,
>   With a bright silver wand.
> Like Julian the Roman,
>   He's one that fears no man.
>
> It's said there's one predestinate
>   To be his mortal foe;
> But that man is yet unborn,
>   And long may it be so."

The young man had not travelled far before he espied another old man, whose locks were worn grey, herding a drove of swine, who, when he asked to whom they belonged, received the same answer as from the shepherd.

At length, he came to a third man herding goats and, upon asking him the same question to whom they belonged, the goat-herder's answer was the same. However, this old man also bade him, "Beware of a parcel of animals which lay before you, for they are of quite a different species from those you have formerly seen."

On coming up to these animals, the young lad discovered they were indeed frightful, having two heads, and on every head four horns, and otherwise were most hideous in their appearance.

He fled from them with all speed, and reached a castle in which he took shelter. After having knocked and entered, he was saluted by an old woman, who sat in a corner of the kitchen by the fire, and asked, "From where do you come?"

Having satisfied her as to his former place of residence, and the cause of leaving his own country, she in return, informed him of the dangers he faced if found in that castle, as it belonged to the Red Etin, a horrid monster with three frightful heads, who spared no man.

"However," she said, "if you can, by any means, devise a

method to secrete yourself from his sight for this night, I will not divulge where."

He did his best to keep himself secure, but it was all in vain, for as soon as the Red Etin came in, he said,

    "I smell a living man,
      And, be he from Fife, or be he from Tweed,
      His heart, this night, shall season my bread."

The young lad was then drawn from his lurking-place, and the Red Etin said, "If you answer the three questions which I will demand of you, you shall be safe. But if you do not, death without redress will be your destiny, and that without delay."

The first question which was put to him was: *Whether Scotland or Ireland was first inhabited?* But this question he was unable to answer.

The second was: *Whether the man was made for the woman, or the woman made for the man?* This question he also was unable to answer correctly.

The third and last question was: *Whether the man or the brutes were made first?* Being unable to answer this one also, he was asked to choose the instrument of death by which he was to suffer.

Having declined anything on the subject, the Red Etin took a mallet and knocked him down, and changed him into a pillar of stone.

The second widow's son having all this time continued at home, began to think of the fate of his former companion, and looked at the knife. Upon finding by its change of colour that its owner had suffered death or confinement, he determined to go in pursuit of his neighbour.

Having acquainted his mother with his plan, she, as the former had done, gave him a broken pitcher to carry water from the well, which was a considerable distance from her house.

In every respect, he was treated as the former, and under the same unfavourable circumstances took his departure. He took the same route as the former traveller had done, and met with the same obstacles, so that his end was no more fortunate.

Sometime after, one of the widows had another son, who had heard of the fate of his brother and neighbour, as his mother had learned their unsuccessful end from a Fairy. This young man then determined to release his brother from confinement if he was alive; or, if dead, to punish his murderer.

His mother endeavoured to prevail upon him to stay at home, but all her persuasions availed her nothing, he was determined to go on his way.

Prior to leaving, he received, as his brother had done, a broken pitcher to bring home water to bake him a loaf of bread. But, as the water streamed out as fast as he put it in, a raven flew over his head and advised him, "Cement it with clay." That being immediately attended to, he thereby brought it home so full that his loaf was very large.

The mother, as on the former occasion, asked him the same question as she had done of her first son, "Will you accept half of this bread with my blessing, or the whole of it with my curse?" This time, however, she received a different answer.

Having a half of a loaf that was yet bigger than the whole that his brother and neighbour had received, and in consequence of receiving his mother's blessing, he was therefore more successful than those who had gone on the same errand before him.

He was some considerable distance from home when he met a diminutive old woman who asked of him, "May I have a small portion of your bread?"

This he most readily granted, remarking at the same time, "There is more than enough for both of us."

For that, she gave him a magical rod, or wand, endowed

with particular virtues; and also, such information as he would find useful, and of the utmost consequence to him, in his journey.

After having cordially taken his leave of her, he went on the rest of his way rejoicing—and she disappeared in an instant.

On coming to the old man herding the sheep, he enquired, as his brother had previously done, "To whom do these sheep belong?"

The young man received an answer somewhat different than the former:

> "The Red Etin of Ireland
>    Once lived in Bellygan,
> And stole King Malcolm's daughter,
>    The King of fair Scotland.
>
> He beats her, he binds her,
>    He lays her in a band;
> And every day he strikes her,
>    With a bright silver wand.
> Like Julian the Roman,
>    He's one that fears no man.
>
> But now I fear his end is near,
>    And destiny at hand;
> And you're to be, I plainly see,
>    The heir of all his land."

Having approached the man attending the swine, he asked the same question as he had formerly done, and received the answer as has been given by the old man tending the sheep.

On coming to the goat-herder, he was told by him, "Beware of the monsters which lay before you in your way."

But, as he was impervious against the threatened danger,

he passed heedlessly on, until one of the beasts approached with open mouth, ready to devour him. He struck it with his wand, and laid it—in an instant—as for dead at his feet.

Coming to the Red Etin's castle, he knocked and was admitted as the former travellers had been. The same old woman, who sat in the corner of the kitchen, warned him, as she had done his brother, of his danger.

She also told him what the fate of his brother and the former traveller had been and where they were to be found, and the manner in which the Red Etin would make his entry—by the rattling of chains, the sounding of trumpets, and other unusual noises.

She requested of him, "Take shelter, if possible, in some secure place, and escape his fury."

But the young man, regardless of her beneficial advice, only stooped a little behind the chair on which the old woman sat, where he was at once discovered by the ferocious Etin, who commanded, "Come before me!"—which he did courageously.

The same three questions were put to him, but answered differently, thanks to the diminutive old woman who gave him the wand. The Etin's power now being gone, an axe was taken up by the young man, with which he cut off the three heads of the monstrous Etin.

His next task was to discover the King of Scotland's daughter, and to set her free. The old woman showed him the place where she lay concealed. There were imprisoned along with her, a great many beautiful Ladies, all of whom he restored to their weeping parents, by whom he was well rewarded, and married by the King to one of the Ladies who had been released from a long and dreary confinement.

He also restored his brother and the former young man to life and their former shape, and married them to two of the liberated Ladies. They all lived happy, in peace and plenty; this happened through the instrumentality of a persevering and fortunate young man.

**Aarne-Thompson-Uther [ATU] Classification of Folk Tales**
II. 300-749: Tales of Magic
   II.i. 300-399: Supernatural Adversaries
      *II.i.iv. 303: The Twins or Blood-Brothers*

## II
## *The Young Prince*

When Scotland was first inhabited, it was governed by several kings, one of whom had married a Princess of great virtue, who had an only son. She died before the boy came of age and the King married another woman, a less virtuous woman than the Princess had been, as she gave proof afterwards by her cruelty to her stepson.

The young Prince, having borne her ill-treatment for a long time, at length determined to leave his father's court, and seek new adventures in a foreign land.

Having at length arrived in a kingdom where there was a young Princess; he made love to her, but she scorned his proffers with high disdain, although in her heart she partly loved him.

After having continued in this kingdom for some time, he received a message from his father to return home, as the Queen, his stepmother, longed to see him, having concealed her hatred for him.

On the arrival of the letter, the Prince consulted his

favourite and faithful servant, whom he justly held in high estimation for his wisdom and fidelity. "Should I obey the mandates of the letter, and return to my father's court, or remain here?"

The servant advised him, "Comply with your father's request, sire, but upon no account should you enter the Queen's apartments, nor taste anything that you might be given to eat or drink, for she certainly has a design upon your life. If a drink is offered to you, make sure to have a hunting-horn by your side that has been constructed to hold whatever is put into it without being observed."

All things being now prepared for his journey homewards, they set off, and on their arrival at his father's palace, the young Prince was hailed with every demonstration of joy, and entreated to come in. This he declined, and excused himself by saying, "I am engaged in a very particular business which shall occupy most of my time on this visit, but I will return shortly after with more leisure."

The Queen then, seeing herself likely to be disappointed in her diabolical purpose, insisted much upon him drinking something before his departure, which at last he consented to do, to prevent any suspicion that might arise from his obstinacy.

She then gave him the poisonous, though fortunately not murderous, draught; but he, being advised of the nature of it beforehand, put it secretly into his hunting-horn and left her.

The Prince and his servant had not gone far when the servant proposed, "Perhaps we should get a cake baked with the liquid, sire, and give it to a dog, to try on him the verity of our suspicion."

This being done, the dog to which the cake was given had no sooner eaten it than he swelled, burst, and died. Three ravenous birds that came and ate the dog's flesh and picked his bones, immediately burst and died. The same fate awaited twenty-four crows that also ate of the flesh. Such was the nature and strength of the poison which this murderous woman had prepared for the young Prince.

Having now left the country, he went a second time to visit his former mistress, the foreign Princess; but on his arrival at her father's court, she still denied him her hand. It was, however, so far agreed upon, that if he would put forth a riddle which she was unable to expound, then would she consent to be his wife.

He then gave her the following: *The horn killed one and that one killed three, and these three killed twenty-four.*

They agreed to a whole day being allowed for her to arise at its solution; but being unable to comprehend its meaning, she soon became very uneasy. One of her Ladies-in-Waiting proposed, "Bribe his servant with a purse of money, milady, to elicit the secret from him."

The Lady-in-Waiting went accordingly to the servant, and with a purse of gold, requested, "Give me the secret and you shall have the money."

But he would not consent to her demand upon any other terms than her lying with him that night. To this condition, she was at first quite averse, but at length consented.

No sooner had the dawn of morning appeared, than she demanded of him the fulfilment of his promise, but he excused himself by saying, "I will give it to none but a maiden."

She insisted that she was one of the Queen's Ladies-in-Waiting, and consequently a maiden. This reasoning, however, was not sufficient for him, after what had so lately passed between them. She had no recourse but to return and inform the Princess of her poor outcome.

A second and a third maiden went on the same errand, but were alike unsuccessful, having been handled in the same manner as the first had been.

At length, the Princess determined to try her own success and set out for the Prince's lodgings. The servant, however, had instructed his master so completely in being able to imitate his voice and mimic his gesture, that the Prince could pass for the servant. And so when the Princess arrived, she, of course, lay with the Prince instead of his servant, as she imagined she had done; but, she still came short of her wished-for knowledge of the horn and the beasts.

When the time appointed came for her to give the explanation of the riddle, the Princess could not, and so had no alternative but to marry the Prince.

He, however, being willing to give her another chance of escaping from the marriage bed, said, "I will give you another riddle, and if you can solve it correctly, then you shall be free from all your former obligations in regards to me."

This being agreed to by all parties concerned, the Prince said: "*Last night, Jack, my man, shot three milk-white swans, and the master-man the master-swan.*"

"Not four, my lord?" she replied.

"No," he answered.

"Then, father," said she, addressing him the King, "it is this Prince that I will have."

They were then accordingly married, and lived for many years in great splendour, while the Prince's miserable stepmother pined and died of a broken heart.

**Aarne-Thompson-Uther [ATU] Classification of Folk Tales**
IV. 850-999: Realistic Tales
   IV.i. 850-869: The Man Marries the Princess
      IV.i.ii. 851: The Riddle of the Suitor

# III
## *The History of Mr Greenwood*

In the Western Isles of Scotland there once lived a very rich man, of the name of Gregory, who had two beautiful daughters, to whom he was inordinately attached; but, being vastly rich, he would not permit either of them to go for an hour out of his presence without a strong detachment of the attendants of his house accompanying them wherever they went. They additionally served the purpose of defending the daughters from violent attacks that might be made upon them, or being carried off by the lawless bandits, who at that time infested that part of the country.

It happened, however, one day when they were at their usual walk and recreation, a little distance from their house, there came up to them a gentleman with his servant on horseback, who accosted them in a rather familiar way, asking them, "Are those men we see at a little distance attendants of yours?"

The Ladies answered in the affirmative.

The gentleman also put some other questions to them,

which they chose not to answer.

The younger of the Ladies spoke, "I wish to know, sir, how you are so impertinent."

When he replied—"I am much attached to your elder sister, for her beauty is so enchanting"—he broke through the rules of good breeding. However, as flattery has too often the desired effect of gaining its purpose over silly minds, it worked upon this Lady like a charm, and made her the more attentive to his bewitching ways.

Having so far gained her heart and confidence, the gentleman next learnt all the information that he wanted regarding her place of residence, and other particulars, with liberty to visit her as a suitor.

These preliminaries having been settled, the Ladies returned home, attended by the gentleman stranger, who gave his name as Mr Greenwood, proprietor of an extensive tract of land on one of the neighbouring Islands.

His visits becoming so frequent, and himself so familiar, that at length he entreated the Lady, his sweetheart, to pay a visit in return to his castle, as it was but a short way off, to which she consented.

The necessary instructions were given to her for finding the castle secretly, as she could not go openly for fear of her father, he not permitting her to go anywhere without her usual guard of attendants. It was necessary, therefore, for her to steal away in his absence.

The time for this assignation was agreed upon—in a few days, when it was expected her father would leave home. But as some secret forebodings of evil preyed much upon her mind, she thought it advisable to go to the place he had appointed some days prior to the time they were to meet.

The impropriety of venturing alone, and to a place she did not know, and to meet with one with whom she was so little acquainted, seemed very improper. So, having deliberately weighed the matter in her own mind, she thought it better to go in disguise and reconnoitre his dwelling and circumstances.

Accordingly, she dressed herself in the tattered and torn clothing of an old beggar woman, and went as proposed, asking alms on her way there.

On her arriving at Greenwood's castle, she knocked loudly, but as no one appeared, she ventured in, as the door was unlocked, and destitute of a bolt for its security.

Her first movement was to examine the contents of a pot which boiled on the fire, but on looking in, she saw such a sight as quite horrified her—it was part of a human body!

Next, she observed a bundle of rusty keys lying upon a table in the kitchen. After picking them up, she applied one of them to the door of a room that adjoined the kitchen.

In this room hung men's clothes of every description. She cut a swatch out of each garment, which having pocketed, she went to another room. Opening it also, she found there women's dresses of great variety; some new, and some old. Out of each of them, she cut again.

Her next adventure was down a small trap-door, where, when she arrived at the bottom, she was up to the knees in blood, at which she greatly wondered. But in the midst of her astonishment, from one of the dark corners of this dreadful vault, a voice said:

"O, dear Lady Maisry, be not so bold,
   Lest your warm heart blood soon turn as cold."

On hearing these words, she immediately fled from this ocean of blood, and ascended with a quick though trembling step, until she arrived at its summit.

On beholding the light, she was put to her wits' end thinking of how she should make her escape from this place of skulls, which she never thought of until now.

On ruminating on these things, her eyes were shocked at the sight of the cannibal owner of the place and his servant dragging triumphantly by the hair of the head, the dead body of a murdered female.

As they came hurriedly into the room upon her, she had little time to seek a hiding place, or meditate her escape; so she fled behind a door which stood half open between them, but so placed that she could hear and see what passed without being observed by the other party.

Near this place lay a large bloodhound, to which she threw a piece of bread and by that means gained his favour. Greenwood then cut off one of the female's hands and threw it to the dog; but as Maisry had so recently given him a piece of bread, she was suffered to take it up and carry it away.

Having continued in this precarious situation for a wearisome length of time, Greenwood remarked to his man, that he smelled fresh blood.

The servant, with some difficulty, managed to persuade him that the smell arose from the hand which he had so recently cut off from the dead body and thrown to the dog. He was also, with some reluctance, appeased in his rage towards one of his domestics that had offended him.

Greenwood, however, determined that on going to bed, all the doors should be well secured inside, so that none could make their escape before morning, if any were in the house that did not belong to it; and for their better security, they should have their beds made at one of the back doors of the castle.

On their going to bed, as fate would have it, sleep took such a strong hold of their senses that they were soon in the arms of the drowsy god and snored aloud.

It was now time for the Lady to think of saving herself by

flight, which she accomplished in a surprising manner: she opened the door, and at once made such a spring over both of their bodies, that she cleared them and the place of her confinement. She then fled with the rapidity of lightning.

The jump which she took awoke Greenwood, who said, "Surely someone has escaped."

But the servant insisted, "It was only the flutter of a bird that has passed by the door."

Unconcerned, they then went to sleep again.

Having reached her father's house, the Lady invited a great party of her friends and acquaintances to a feast, which was to be prepared for their entertainment, about the time that Greenwood had promised to call upon her.

All things being ready, the guests arrived for supper, Greenwood among the rest. All were merry, seeming to enjoy the entertainment.

When supper ended, it was proposed that a few songs, for the amusement of the company, should be sung by those who could, and those who could not sing should tell some story or tale.

This being agreed upon by all, songs were sung and tales were told by all until it came to Maisry's turn, who said, "As I can do neither, I will tell a dream I dreamed last night," and looking over to Greenwood, remarked that it concerned him.

All seemed anxious to hear it, but none more so than Greenwood, when she began speaking. "I thought that I disguised myself as a common pauper, and went to your castle to ask alms. But after loudly knocking, and finding no one to make answer, I ventured in, and seeing a pot boiling on the fire, a thought struck me to look into it. I saw what I could scarcely believe—a part of a human body!

"This having raised my curiosity, I went a step further, and on finding a bunch of keys lying on a table near where I stood, I opened a door near the kitchen, and found a variety of men's clothes. Next, I opened another, where I found women's clothes and cut a piece out of each of them, which I brought along.

"I also ventured down a small trap-stair, when I found myself up to the knees among blood, and a voice saying:

> 'O, dear Lady Maisry, be not so bold,
> Lest your warm heart blood soon turn as cold.'"

Greenwood could contain himself no longer, and interrupting her said, "Women's dreams are fabulous, and so are women's thoughts. Jack, saddle your horse, and we will go ride."

But she would not consent to this, and continued to tell the rest of her dream, much against his wish or inclination; but there was no avoiding hearing her out, so she went on.

"On arriving at the top of the trap-stair, which I went down to the vault of blood, I observed you and your man dragging by the hair of her head, the body of a dead lady. You cut off one of her hands and threw it to a greedy bloodhound which lay near where I stood. The hand I took up, and see here it is," she said, producing the bloody hand before them all.

At that moment, to his mortification and confusion, Greenwood and his servant were secured. He was to be burned in the midst of his castle, which was in a remote and secret place of a large wood; his servant was to be drowned. These judgments were immediately carried out, to the no small satisfaction and amazement of all who heard his murderous history.

**Aarne-Thompson-Uther [ATU] Classification of Folk Tales**
IV. 850-999: Realistic Tales
    IV.viii. 950-969: Robbers and Murderers
        *IV.viii.vi. 955: The Robber Bridegroom*

## IV
### *The Cruel Stepmother*

About the year 800, there lived a rich nobleman in a sequestered part of Scotland, where he wished to conceal his name, birth, and parentage, as he had fled from the hands of justice to save his life for an action he had been guilty of committing in his early years.

It was supposed, and not without some good show of reason, that his name was Malcolm, brother to Fingal, King of Morven. Be this as it may, it so happened that he had chosen a pious and godly woman for his consort; who, on giving birth to a daughter, Beatrix, soon after departed this life.

Malcolm—as we shall call him, for the better understanding of his history—lived as a widower for the space of sixteen years, when he got to thinking that his daughter was now of such an age that she would leave him, if she got a good offer.

With his head full of these thoughts, he went to a distant part of the country where the Thane of Mull dwelt, and made love to one of his daughters, whom he afterwards married and brought to his own domain.

The new bride had no sooner fixed her eyes on Beatrix, than she conceived the most deadly hatred imaginable; so much so, that it almost deprived her of her rest, deliberating on schemes of how to get rid of her stepdaughter, as she envied her for her superior beauty.

One day, on a day her husband was going hunting, she took the young Lady and bound her by an oath that whatever she saw or heard her do or say, she would conceal from her father—the oath being extorted from Beatrix by threatening her with death and destruction, if she did not comply.

The first act of the stepmother was to go into the garden and cut down a favourite tree, which was in full blossom, and destroy the root and beauty of the branches by burning them.

On Malcolm's return, he immediately discovered the absence of his favourite tree, and got into such a passion, few could approach the place where he was for a considerable length of time.

When his passion had somewhat subsided, he asked his wife, "What has become of my favourite tree? How has it been destroyed?"

She desired him to ask his daughter, adding, "As I know nothing about it myself."

Beatrix was then summoned before him and interrogated, with all the rigour of a passionate father, as to her knowledge of the destruction of his favourite tree.

Her only answer was, "He who is above knows all about it." No more satisfaction would she give him.

A second time, he went from home, and on his return, Malcolm found his favourite hound weltering in his blood. This again renewed his passion, but who was the guilty person he could never learn; on enquiring at his daughter, he received the same answer as before.

A third time, he went hunting, and on his return, Malcolm found his favourite hawk lying dead; but the perpetrators of these horrid deeds he could not discover. On applying to his wife, he was requested to ask his daughter; and on consulting her, her answer was as at the first.

Seeing that all the stratagems which she had devised for her destruction had proved fruitless, his wife—to gratify her mortal hatred, rather than suffer her to live—would sacrifice everything she had in the world.

One year had scarcely passed in this disagreeable manner, when the Lady delivered a fine boy, which soon became the darling of his father. This was too glaring not to be easily perceived by the mother; but rather than live the life which she had done since they had been married, with the envious venom rankling in her breast, she would destroy her own child and offspring.

This being determined upon, one night, when Beatrix was in bed sleeping soundly, dreading no harm, this bad woman, her stepmother, took a knife, bereaved the sweetly smiling young boy of his life, and laid him—with the knife reeking in gore—into the arms of the innocent Beatrix.

After having been in bed for some time with her husband, she started as from some frightful dream, crying, "Oh, my child! What has become of my lovely child?"

This alarmed Malcolm, who, on looking for the boy, did not find him.

The mother then said, "I am much afraid that Beatrix has stolen him away from us while we slept, and has murdered him."

The father, by no means, could be made to believe this; but upon examining her bed, the boy was discovered mangled, and the knife beside him.

Malcolm was now petrified with horror, and could ask

nor answer anything.

It was in vain that the young Lady pleaded ignorance, and denied the guilty deed, for the proofs were too strong—as certainly no one could have suspected the unnatural mother of such cruel barbarity—and no one else had access to the place where it lay but Beatrix.

Her father then determined to put her to the cruellest torture for the death of his beloved child, and she was charged with all the other bad deeds which had been committed for the space of the past twelve months in his house and premises.

He took her to a wood, and after having cut off her right hand and arm, he next cut off her right leg. She still pleaded her innocence, but rather than perjure herself, she would suffer all that he chose to inflict upon her.

However, as proof of her innocence, she told him, "On your way homewards, a thorn will stick in your foot that none but myself can extract, and that only after my arm and leg have been reunited with my body as before."

He paid no attention to this, but next cut out her tongue, and left her to perish, or to be destroyed by wild beasts in the wood.

She had not, however, lain long in this humiliating posture, when a Knight came riding that way. On observing her, he alighted from his horse and enquired as to the nature of her sufferings.

As Beatrix could not speak, she made signs to him for pen, ink, and paper, when she wrote an account of the whole. He then took her on his horse behind him and carried her home to his mother, who—being acquainted with the virtues of the water of a particular well nearby—soon restored to her the full use of her amputated limbs, but her tongue continued still to be useless.

The Knight, notwithstanding the deficiency of the want of

her tongue and speech, took such a liking to Beatrix that shortly after they were married, and lived in the greatest peace and pleasure, until one day when it was necessary for him to leave his country on some very urgent business.

Prior to his setting off, he had matters so arranged, that by giving certain directions to his wife, she might write to him by her Page. All things being prepared, the Knight went away with a sorrowful heart.

He had not been long away when his wife, being pregnant, became sick at heart and longed to see her esteemed lord. A message was then sent to the place of his residence with a request that he would return immediately home.

The messenger was her own Page, who was directed to make every dispatch, and not to tarry on the way; but these instructions he soon forgot when out of sight and reach of his mistress.

As he journeyed on his way, it so happened that he took up his abode for the night in the very house of Beatrix's father. Malcolm's wife, observing the stranger, was desirous of knowing his errand, and so prevailed upon him to give her a glimpse of the letter which he carried from Beatrix to her husband.

By her fair speeches, she so won his heart, that the Page gave it to her. On opening it, she soon discovered from whom it came, and tore it, and wrote in its place one, as if came from his mother, requesting him to put away or destroy the bad woman he had brought unto her.

To this letter the Knight made no reply, when a second one was written by his wife, not knowing the cause of his delay; but it shared the same fate as the former, and another of like tenor—breathing the bitterest enmity and hatred against his beloved and virtuous wife—put in its place.

On receiving this second menacing letter, the Knight

hurried home, and finding his wife in the house, without any provocation or enquiry, he immediately dragged her outside, and abused her very unmercifully, until having driven her into a ditch to get quit of her altogether, a powerful herb happened to get into her mouth in the course of her struggle, which at once restored to her the use of her speech.

It now became her turn to interrogate him, and she asked him, "Why have you used me so cruelly, without a cause?"

He then showed her the letters which he had received purporting to be from his mother.

Beatrix said, "These were not written by your mother, for we live on the most friendly terms imaginable."

The letters were then referred to his mother, who, on seeing them, was no less surprised than vexed at them, and at his maltreating his wife so contemptibly.

The Page was then called and examined, at which point he confessed to what he had done.

The Knight, without further enquiry into the matter, took his sword and cut off the Page's head, and threw it away, as a warning to all others not to betray their trust, but behave in a more upright and honourable manner.

At length, it was discovered that the cruel stepmother had been the sole cause of the whole of Beatrix's misfortunes, and she was adjudged to be put to an ignominious death by the cruellest torture, which was carried out immediately after, as a just reward for her hatred and cruelty.

Beatrix then relieved her father from the pain which he suffered in his foot by way of a thorn that was stuck in it, and baffled all the medical skill in that part of the country. Afterwards, they lived to a good old age and died in peace.

**Aarne-Thompson-Uther [ATU] Classification of Folk Tales**
II. 300-749: Tales of Magic

II.vii. 700-749: Other Tales of the Supernatural
 *II.vii.v. 706: The Maiden Without Hands*

# V
## *Rashen Coatie*

In an early period, when a plurality of Kings reigned in Scotland, it chanced that one of them had lost his Queen; and one of the Queens had lost her husband. These two, the widow and widower were married, each of them having had a daughter in their first marriage, it caused a good deal of dissension and strife, particularly as the King's daughter was a perfect model of beauty, and the Queen's daughter as much so of deformity.

But the King was willing to indulge his Queen as much as possible, and for the sake of keeping peace in his own house, he often winked at the bad treatment his daughter received from her stepmother, all because she was more handsome and fair than her beloved but ugly daughter.

Her treatment was so very bad, however, that she was put to herding her father's cattle; while the Queen's daughter wallowed in all the luxuries of a court endowed with peace and plenty. The meat brought daily to her by the Queen's favourite daughter was of the coarsest fare; however, Rashin Coatie—for so shall the King's daughter be called—had learned from some kind Fairy how to charm her stepsister asleep when partaking of her food, which she did on her immediate arrival, by repeating the following words:

> "Lay down your head upon my knee,
> And well looked after it there shall be,
> Then sleep you one eye or sleep you two,
> You soon shall see what power can do."

These words had the desired effect of lulling her stepsister sound asleep, which had no sooner taken place than a Genii—in the shape and form of a calf—brought her meats and dainties of every description, of which she partook heartily, unknown to all but her favourite calf.

The Queen being now wearied with trying all the arts that mischief could devise to bring Rashen Coatie's beauty to a level with her daughter's, or to raise her daughter's beauty to that of Rashen Coatie's, thought her stepdaughter must have some hidden means of subsistence, as all the stratagems she tried always resulted in a lack of success.

On consulting her henwife—who was a witch—about how she should behave in this critical juncture, the witch said, "I will give you an eye in her neck, by which sight you will be able to discover many things, particularly how Rashen Coatie is fed and maintained, without her perceiving it."

Accordingly, the Queen went the next day to the castle to discover Rashen Coatie's friends, and discovered how she was fed, owing to an omission of Rashen Coatie's. She found that it was the calf that fed her, which made the Queen long to get it destroyed.

Though the King was loath to deprive his daughter of her only companion, her favourite calf, he was obliged to comply with the Queen's imperious demands, in order to suppress the wrangling and strife, which were daily taking place among his domestics, particularly by his Queen.

Having discovered the Queen's intention, Rashen Coatie mourned over her ravenous appetite, with streaming eyes and bleached cheeks.

The calf, having the power of speech, requested of her, "Do not be alarmed at what is to take place. Instead, gather together all my bones into one mass, and place them beneath that particular stone. In a short time, they will revive and come to life again."

Rashen Coatie having done as commanded, everything came to pass as predicted by the calf; and the malicious Queen, having partaken of the entrails of the calf, lingered and died of a disease unknown of in that part of the country.

The Queen's daughter now became an object of contempt, despised and dismissed by everyone. Rashen Coatie's sun now began to shine in meridian splendour; she was gentle and mild, humble to everyone, which gained her the esteem and goodwill of both great and small.

Her beauty having kept pace with her virtue, her father took such a liking to her, as to wish to marry her; but this being quite contrary to her principles of sound morality, she grew melancholy, every day more and more, and lingered out a weary existence, until she met with her calf and asked, "What is to be done under such pressing difficulties? What is the best way forward for me?"

The calf advised her, "Ask your father for a gown and petticoat made of the rushes that grow on the side of the bonny burn." This having been accomplished, she then requested that he give her a dress composed of all the colours of the birds of the air. This also having been given to her, she demanded a new set of clothes of variegated colours, composed of all those appearances that float in the air, and the earth beneath.

Having obtained all these varieties, she now had no

excuse but to comply with her father's wishes, which were to accompany him to the altar, where all things were ready for the marriage ceremony.

Having thus far complied with his wishes, she went, but on arriving at the appointed place, she started back, exclaiming, "I have forgotten my marriage ring!"

Her father, to prevent her returning home, said, "I have one which will fit the purpose perfectly well."

But Rashen Coatie insisted on having her mother's ring, and that she needed to return for it, but promised to be back in a few minutes.

Again, she had the opportunity to seek advice from her calf, who said, "Dress yourself in your coat of rushes and leave your father's kingdom with all speed."

This was accordingly done, and she wandered far until she came to a hunting lodge, kept by the Prince of that country. Here she made free to enter, and went to the Prince's bed to rest her wearied limbs, which had undergone much toil and fatigue in the course of a long and laborious journey.

When the Prince came to his lodge, he was surprised to find a sleeping beauty in his bed, as it was in an isolated part of his kingdom, where few inhabitants were to be found.

Rashen Coatie soon made her escape from him, and went to his father's palace, where she asked for a position as a menial servant, which was granted, and thereby put into the kitchen to assist the cook in turning the spits which groaned with the weight of the meat that was roasting for their majesties' dinner.

Here she continued for some time, doing all the drudgery of the lowliest servant. Christmas, however, came on, when great preparations were made for church. Rashen Coatie also wished to appear among the rest, but was denied permission by the Master Cook.

But it so happened that, on the first day of Yule, when all were gone, and she was left alone in the kitchen to attend the meat, she said to the spits, peats, and pots, to do their duty until she returned, which was done accordingly—the words of the charm that she made use of on this occasion were:

> "Every spit make another turn,
> Every peat make another burn,
> Every pot make another play
> Till I return on good Yule day."

These did as desired, while she went and dressed herself in rich attire. On arriving at the church, she placed herself in a conspicuous part of the seating, nearly opposite to where the young Prince was sitting.

He caught more of the flame of love than of the minister's spiritual exhortations, and could scarcely contain himself from making enquiries during the sermon.

She went in the same manner all the holy days of Yule, but every day more and more superbly dressed. The Prince at length determined on discovering her rank and place of abode, if possible, little thinking that it was his own menial, Rashen Coatie, as her history seemed to be a mystery to everyone.

However, the term of her secrecy seemed to be now at an end, for hurrying home on the last day, she dropped one of her shoes, which were so completely fitted to her feet that it was supposed it would suit no one else.

The Prince, on having found the shoe, which was of pure gold, caused to be proclaimed throughout all the regions of his father's kingdom round about, that everyone should have free liberty to try on the shoe, and whomsoever the shoe fitted best, was to be his bride.

Many trials were made, but all to no purpose, until the henwife's daughter caused her heels and toes to be pared; by which process she forced the shoe onto her foot.

In accordance with the proclamation, it therefore became the Prince to marry her, with which he was to comply, though it was with a heavy heart.

On their way to the marriage seat, a small bird fluttered over their heads, crying as they went:

"Clipped heels and pared toes.
They're in the kitchen the shoe on goes."

Hearing the voice of the bird, the Prince requested to know its meaning, which was explained to him. With joy, the Prince returned to his father's castle—much against the henwife's inclination—and it was soon discovered that Rashen Coatie, who crouched in the kitchen, had not been given the opportunity of trying on the shoe.

On presenting her with the shoe, it went easily on; but what was more, to their surprise and astonishment, she pulled out its fellow and put it on before them.

Rashen Coatie and the Prince, of course, we need not add, were immediately married, and lived long and happy lives together. Shortly after their marriage, they paid a visit to her father's court in great pomp and grandeur, by whom they were most cordially received, and his kingdom, at his death, was bestowed on them.

**Aarne-Thompson-Uther [ATU] Classification of Folk Tales**
II. 300-749: Tales of Magic
   II.iv. 500-559: Supernatural Helpers
      II.iv.ix. 510: Cinderella and Catskin
         II.iv.ix.ii. B: Unnatural Love
      II.iv.x. 511: One-Eye, Two-Eyes, and Three-Eyes

# VI
## *The Brown Bull of Ringlewood*

When old King Coil lived, he had three pretty daughters, on whom he greatly doted, and his chief enjoyment was in seeing them happy. It so happened one day, while he was walking for his recreation, that he met with an old man in apparently decayed circumstances, who asked charity of him, for the King was well known for his benevolence to all those in need.

On receiving alms, the poor man said, "I am not an earthly person, but merely assumed such an appearance to test your generosity. Having found you liberal and kind, I will reward you with any three wishes you can think of. Or, as you have three beautiful daughters, it might be more agreeable to you to give each of them a wish." This the old man promised to see accomplished.

Having parted with this stranger, the King wondered as he went home if what the old man had promised would ever come to pass. On arriving at his palace, he told his oldest daughter, in a jocular manner, "Wish for your heart's desire, and you shall have it, whatever it may be." He went to his other two daughters and told them the same.

No sooner had the oldest daughter been informed of this than she wished the King of Westmoreland to come and marry her; which was no sooner wished for than done, as he carried her off to his kingdom.

The second daughter, having seen the efficacy of her sister's wish, immediately wished that the King of Southland would come and marry her; this also was done swiftly to the satisfaction of all concerned.

The King now asked his youngest daughter what she wished for; when, in a jesting manner, she said, "I wish that the Brown Bull of Ringlewood would come and carry me off."

She had scarcely uttered the words when the Bull appeared, and, having mounted her on his horns, immediately carried her off to his castle. Upon their arrival, he disappeared, but at night he returned to the castle—having metamorphosed into the figure and shape of a man—and lay down beside her.

He continued departing from the castle in the morning, and returning in the evening, for the duration of three years, during which time the young Princess bore him three beautiful sons.

Having wearied of this way of living, she at length ventured to ask an old woman who frequented the castle, "Why does my husband assume the appearance of a Brown Bull through the day, but came home as a handsome young man at night?"

The old woman instructed her to burn the Bull's hide, which lay above his bed, some morning before he got out of his bed. Having done as directed, the skin went out of the chimney with a noise like thunder.

The young Prince, for so he was, immediately woke from his slumber. He then rose from his bed, and told the Princess,

"It is time for me to depart to a faraway country."

She asked him, "To what place do you belong?"

"My father is King of a country far beyond the sea," he told her, "to which I intend to go immediately, for I have been kept by some magical power in the shape and likeness which you have seen me take for many years, but now the charm has broken."

The Princess wished to accompany him there, which he agreed to, but desired her never to look behind, or she would forget all that had passed.

At length, they arrived at a most beautiful hill, pure as crystal and as transparent as air, which was called the Hill of Forgetfulness. On arriving at this hill, the Princess could not, by any means, contrive how to ascend it. He, therefore, requested her,

> "To look between you and the sky,
> And there you will a castle spy."

Into this castle he desired her to put one of their boys, where he would be well educated, clothed, and fed.

In the same manner, he requested of her to look east and west, and she would see other castles, into which she would put their other two sons.

Having ascended the hill himself, the Prince entirely forgot her, so that she was obliged to go and serve seven years as a cook to a nobleman that lived close by the Hill of Forgetfulness before he would give her any assistance to mount the hill.

Her task having been accomplished, the people of the castle whom she had served, provided her with everything necessary for her journey, which on receiving, she went away rejoicing, and ascended the hill with ease.

On reaching the top, she met with an old woman who requested that she pull for her three of the pears that hung on a tree in the midst of a garden through which she had to pass.

"If you do so," the old woman said, "I shall reward you with three eggs which will be of the utmost consequence to you in your subsequent life, if well managed. You are not, however, to open them upon every emergency, upon any consideration whatever, but to wait patiently until you are beset by grave hardship and see no other way of accomplishing your designed purpose."

Having obtained the three wonderful eggs, the Princess went in pursuit of lodging. Upon applying for lodging at the King's palace, she was told, "As the young Prince is to be married soon, you cannot be accommodated here." All around her was bustle and confusion.

On hearing this, the Princess was greatly cast down; but recollecting herself, she broke one of her eggs, out of which sprang a little wheel spinning gold yarn.

At this instant, the Queen was passing by, and she requested to have the wheel; but upon no other terms would the young Princess part with it than for a night with the young Prince.

This she was denied; but as no other thing could persuade the Princess to sell the wheel, the Queen at last consented, but gave the Prince such a powder, and enchanted bedclothes, that during the night he never wakened; and so the Princess' labour was lost.

The second night came, and when the Princess broke the second egg, there came out a reel, spinning gold yarn. The Queen spied it also, and got it on the same terms as the little wheel.

The third egg was broken, out of which came a singing bird. The Queen needed to be the purchaser of it, as with the other two; and the Princess consented on the former terms.

At length, a bird told the Princess to take the bedclothes

and throw them all to the foot of the bed, after which the Prince would immediately awaken.

This having been done, the Prince awoke from his drowsy slumber, and on recognising his former consort, he renewed his former love and obligations to her, and promised her his hand in a public manner.

He then caused a large chair to be placed in the midst of the palace, intimating that whoever filled it best was to be his wife. This caused many to try it but all in vain, until his former Princess made the same attempt, when she sat down in it with ease, and graced it.

Immediately afterwards, the Prince set her sons beside her, one on each side, and the youngest on her knee. They were then publicly married, and lived happily ever after.

**Aarne-Thompson-Uther [ATU] Classification of Folk Tales**
II. 300-749: Tales of Magic
    II.ii. 400-459: Supernatural or Enchanted Wife, Husband or Other Relative
        II.ii.ii. 425-449: Husband
            II.ii.ii.i. 425: The Search for the Lost Husband
                *II.ii.ii.i.i. A: The Animal as Bridegroom*

# VII
## *The Thriftless Wife*

There once lived, in a place not much frequented in the north of Scotland, a very honest and industrious family, who had one daughter, whose beauty was such that many suitors came to court her; but being of a thoughtless and simple disposition, her mother endeavoured to get her married to the first good offer, which happened soon after this resolution was made.

A young man came a-wooing her, as several had done before him, but he was the most successful, as her mother wished to encourage his suit, and caused the daughter to lay aside her distaff at which she was spinning, and converse a little with her fond lover, who had come to court and call her his own.

Having laid aside her distaff, at which she was so busy, her mother took the young man and her through various parts of the house and showed him the great quantities of yarn which her fond daughter had spun.

In the process of time, the young couple were married, he

thinking himself fortunate in meeting with such a beautiful and industrious helpmate—as beauty and industry are seldom to be found in one person—and she in having met with such a kind and indulgent husband.

The time, however, arrived when each was to try their partner's temper and dispositions, and also their management of household affairs. On arriving at her husband's dwelling, shortly after the marriage, he showed her a great quantity of wool he had to spin and requested that it might be done without loss of time.

However, instead of doing it herself, she gave it all out to her neighbours to spin, who were to receive for hire, each of them a parcel of the wool, and that before the work was finished; so that out of the large parcel given out, none returned but one trifling clew.

One day, her husband asked her, "Is the web finished?"

"The yarn is spun, and next it will be woven," she told him. "In the meantime, it is necessary for you to stay this evening at home, to get it winded upon clews."

To this, he readily consented, happy to have such a task imposed upon him. She cunningly devised the plan of putting him to one end of the house, and—staying herself in the other—she rolled the ball of worsted backwards and forwards on the floor for the whole evening, making him believe at the time it was so many additional clews of the yarn she had spun that he had seen and handled.

Next morning, she arose by break of day and went to see her father, who was a weaver, and told him her pitiful story, and how she had beguiled her husband with the yarn.

Her father, loath to expose her, said, "As I have a web of cloth in the loom, which belongs to me, you should have it, but only if you will behave better in future."

Having got the web on her back, she began her journey

home. She then came to an alehouse on the roadside, where—having stopped a little while to refresh herself—she got rather intoxicated, so that on her coming out of the alehouse, she espied some trees, and in order to see how the web would appear on them, she wrapped one of them around, and sat herself down, and fell fast asleep.

A pedlar came that way and, after having cut off her yellow hair, he took the cloth and went merrily on his way.

On her awakening, she went home in amazement, crying, "Where am I now?"

"Where," said her husband, "but in your own house, where you ought to be. But where is the web?"

"My mother," said she, "told me when I got it on my back, that I would be as braw as John's wife; so I tried how it would look on one of the trees—but I suppose that they have swallowed it or hid it from me."

Her husband then, in a fit of despair, cried out, "I must leave you!"

But she begged him, "Pray, husband, please continue with me. I will do better."

Next, he told her, "I am to kill a sheep for meat for us, and I hope you will not be foolish with it."

After killing the sheep, he commanded, "A bit should be put on for dinner, as I have divided it into as many pieces as there are stocks of kale in the yard."

On his leaving the house, she went and laid to each stock in the garden, a piece of the meat.

When he came home to dinner, seeing a number of birds and beasts collected together in the yard, he asked her, "What have you done?" and was informed of her behaviour on this occasion, which so enraged him that he could scarcely refrain from beating her. But having a swine to kill, he would refrain that time, in the hope that she would do better in the next instance.

The swine was slaughtered, and the greater part of it laid aside for what he called '*Lent and the Lang Reed*' (a holy day on which a feast was to be held), which she mistook for some poor old man, and she asked every beggar their name, until one beggar—more cunning than the rest—informed her that he was the person of whom she had so long sought after, and so got the pig on his back and departed.

When her husband returned from his daily toil at the plough, she told him, with her heart full of glee, "*Lent and the Lang Reed* has been here and has got his portion of the bacon," which again so vexed him to the heart that he was determined to leave her.

Yet, once more, her bitter tears and pitiful supplications softened his heart and made him once more relinquish his project of abandoning her forever, still flattering himself that she would improve in wisdom.

He then informed her, "I have a quantity of oatmeal at the mill, and I trust that you will go and winnow it, and be particularly careful that none of it is lost."

She promised faithfully to do as he wished, but as bad fortune haunted all her actions, she was again unfortunate; for having gone to make ready some food for him with part of the oatmeal, a flea, unluckily, made its entrance into the barrel among the oatmeal.

As she took the whole lot outside of the house to be sifted, and to catch the flea, the wind arose, and blew it all against the garden wall and the walls of the house, which appeared as if they had been newly covered with snow, although this was in the middle of the summer, when everything else was green.

When her husband returned, he found the house and ground all white, which caused him to remark, "There has been a great fall of snow here since I went away this morning."

She gave him an explanation of the whole incident, and he said, "I am now quite ruined, and can stay no longer with you, having tried every scheme and plan that man or wisdom can devise."

They, however, made up matters once more, and he continued a little longer, saying, "I have some hurly-burly seed to sow, and you must be careful of it." So saying, he took a jar and dug a hole in the floor, and put in the jar with the hurly-burly seed—which he said it was, but it was, in fact, true gold.

The word of her foolishness having spread through a great part of the country, a packman came to offer her some finery for dresses, but she said, "I have nothing to give for them, except for a jarful of hurly-burly seed, which has been hidden by my husband, in the midst of the floor."

The packman, being cunning, requested to see it, and knowing its value, offered her what she wanted for it, which she readily accepted, and gave away the jarful of gold for a parcel of childish toys.

On her husband's return, she informed him of her good bargain, but was surprised to see him fly in a rage, exclaiming, "I am now forever done, ruined outright, and will not stay a moment longer, for no persuasion nor another!"

He then went away, but she followed, crying as she went; so, to delay her progress as much as possible from following after him, he told her, "Bring the house door along with you on your back," and she complied.

They travelled hard all that day, and at night found themselves in the midst of a wood, in a remote part of the country. In order to avoid being devoured by wild beasts, they clambered up into the thicket of a lofty tree, right above a robber's retreat.

Having continued for some time in this critical situation,

she wearied with the door on her back—which she had contrived to take up into the tree, along with herself—and she let it fall with such a tremendous crash on the top of the robbers' hut, as made them suspect all was not right above.

They then immediately fled, leaving all their gold and other valuables, with a well-plenished table, behind them.

One of the robbers, however, rather unwilling to part with so much wealth, loitered behind, but he was seized by the throat, and his tongue cut out by the root, by the husband of the foolish woman, as by this time he had descended from the tree.

The robber, having at length brought about his escape, ran after his associates, crying, "Bide! Bide!" But his mouth being full of blood, and his tongue cut out, they who heard him, knew from his cry that he had been in very great danger, and instead of thinking he called to them, as he ran after them, to "Bide! Bide!" thought he cried "Ride! Ride!" So all of them made the best of their escape.

The heartbroken farmer loaded his foolish wife and himself with the spoils of their discovery and went home to their own place, and she reforming her ways, they ended their days in plenty and peace.

**Aarne-Thompson-Uther [ATU] Classification of Folk Tales**
VI. 1200-1999: Anecdotes and Jokes
    VI.iv. 1525-1724: Stories About a Man
        VI.iv.i. 1525-1639: The Clever Man
            *VI.iv.i.xi. 1541: For the Long Winter*
        VI.iv.ii. 1640-1674: Lucky Accidents
            *VI.iv.ii.vi. 1653: The Robbers Under a Tree*

## VIII
### *Green Sleeves*

There once was a King that dwelt in Scotland who had a son that delighted greatly in gambling, and his chief amusement was that of skittles. Having practised it a good deal, he became so dextrous a player that no one could be found to contend with him.

One day, however, as he went out alone, regretting the lack of a partner, an old man appeared, and offered to play with him on the following terms: that, whoever won the game should have it in his power to ask of the other whatever he pleased, and the loser to be strictly bound to the observance of the same, under pain of death.

This being mutually agreed to, they began. The old man was more successful than the Prince and won the game. At this, the Prince was a good deal disconcerted, and said, "You are the first person in Scotland who has ever beaten me."

The terms of the game, as before explained, were that the loser was bound to do whatever was asked by the gainer. The old man then commanded the Prince to tell him his name and place of abode before that day twelve months, or to suffer death.

Upon hearing these hard requests, the Prince went home and went to bed, but would tell no one the cause of his anguish, although often interrogated by his nearest relations.

At length the King, his father, demanded to know the nature of his complaint, and commanded him to inform him immediately, which he did as already related, namely that an old man, with whom he had played a game at skittles, had commanded him to be able to tell him his name and the place of his abode, before the end of the year, being the terms on which they had played.

The King then said, "It would be better to go in pursuit of these particulars than lie desponding on a bed of sickness."

In accordance with his father's advice, the Prince arose the next morning, and travelled the longest summer day in June, until he came to a cottage, at the end of which, on a turf seat, sat an old man, who addressed the Prince familiarly saying, "Well, my Prince, you have come seeking that rogue Green Sleeves. But although I am upwards of two hundred years old, I never saw him but twice, and a little while ago, he passed this house.

"I cannot, however, tell you where he dwells, but my brother who stays two hundred miles farther off, and is four hundred years older than I am, perhaps can tell you, and if you will stay the night at my house, I will put you on a plan to go to him quickly."

The Prince took lodging accordingly and was well entertained. On the morrow, he was led to an adjoining house, and given by the cottager, a round ball with a pair of slippers. He was to roll the ball before him, and the slippers would follow. On arriving at the brother's cottage, he was to give the slippers and ball a kick, at which they would return to their rightful owner.

The Prince accordingly went as directed, and found the second old man sitting by his own door, who said, "Well, Prince, I see you have found me, and I know whom you seek—it is that scoundrel Green Sleeves. You have been at my brother's, but I cannot tell you where he stays more than he does.

"But I shall give you another pair of slippers and a ball, which will take you to another brother that lives about eight hundred miles off, and is about a thousand years older. He will likely be able to tell you where he dwells."

The Prince, as formerly, went again on his adventure, and found the old man, who seemed rather sulky, saying, "I know what you want, and if you will stay with me until tomorrow, I will endeavour to put you upon a plan to find Green Sleeves out."

When tomorrow came, the Prince was taken to a different apartment of the house where he had slept, and addressed by the old man as follows: "Three of Green Sleeves' daughters come to the River Ugie to bathe under the disguise of swans' feathers. You will get behind a hedge of the black sloeberry tree, and there you will be able to observe their motions without being seen.

"As soon as they have stripped themselves of their swan-skins and laid them down, there is one with a blue wing, which you will immediately take up and retain."

The Prince went as directed, and hid behind the blackthorn hedge, when he saw three of the most beautiful swans come and hover over the river for a little time. At length, when they alighted and threw off their swan-skins, he snatched up the one with the blue wing.

After they had continued for some time in the water, they prepared to proceed directly home; but as the one who had the skin with the blue wing could not find hers, she was at a loss as to what to do, more particularly as the other two told her they would not wait, but go on home without her.

On looking wistfully around her, she spied the Prince, whom she knew, and asked him if he had her swan-skin. "I dare not venture to do this," she said, "but upon you immediately giving up my swan-skin, I will help you in how to discover the place of Green Sleeves' retreat, if you will follow my directions."

The Prince then gave her the swan-skin, and she directed him as follows: "First you will come to a river which you will easily cross, but the second will appear more difficult, as it will be raging and foaming up from the bottom. This you must not heed, but venture in, when I will stand by you, and cause a wind to blow upon your clothes, which will immediately dry them."

He found the waters as described, but got more easily over them than he imagined, as he was attended by the Lady, who whistled him over and dried his clothes agreeably to the contract.

On his arriving at the opposite shore, the Prince spied a castle, which he took to be the residence of Green Sleeves. He walked round and round the castle, but could find no entrance. At one of the corners, he discovered a little bell, which he rang, and which brought to his view the porter, who sullenly asked, "What do you want?"

The Prince replied, "What I want is Green Sleeves."

Green Sleeves next made his appearance, and said, "Well, my Prince, you have at length found me out."

On being invited into the castle, the Prince espied an old woman sitting among the ashes, whom Green Sleeves commanded, "Hag, rise immediately and let the Prince sit down!"

The old woman did as required, but the dust that flew from her clothes was likely to smother the Prince. Green Sleeves next commanded her to go and give the Prince some meat; however, she brought him a few fish skins and old mouldy bread, which he said his delicate stomach could not use.

Green Sleeves replied, "No matter, you can go to bed without supper, as you have to rise in the morning and do the job I have for you."

Upon going to bed, the Prince discovered that it was composed of pieces of broken glass, such as bottles and the like, which prevented him from lying down, as the more he attempted to clear the rubbish, it accumulated all the more.

But on looking around him, he spied Blue Wing through a small aperture in the door, who bade him, "Cheer up and be not afraid, as I will be your friend and assist you in your time of need."

And, as proof of the reality of her promise, she immediately transformed his apartment into one of the finest rooms imaginable, with a soft and easy bed for his accommodation.

In the morning, when the Prince arose, everything appeared as it was before, so that, when Green Sleeves appeared and asked him how he had slept, the Prince told him, "It is impossible for anyone to sleep on such a bed. I consider my treatment very harsh. If I had gained the game," he added, "I would not have used you so cruelly."

Green Sleeves, however, persisted in giving him another task to perform, which he thought would not be in the power of man to accomplish, and that was to build a house about a thousand miles long, as many broad, and as many high, to be covered with feathers of every kind of bird that flew; and to have a stone in it out of every quarry in the world, and to be ready before twelve o'clock the next day; or it was to cost him his life.

On hearing of this, the Prince was greatly distressed, and knew not what to do, at which point Blue Wing appeared and requested him not to do anything towards the construction of it, as it was impossible for him to accomplish it alone.

She then opened a box, out of which emerged some thousands of Fairies, who immediately commenced working, and had the house all finished before the time appointed by Green Sleeves, who appeared and remarked, "You have finished my task as commanded, therefore you will go home to your supper and bed, as I have another task for you to perform on the morrow."

The Prince's supper and bed were composed of the same substance as before, and, as before, Blue Wing appeared and changed both into what were more suitable and agreeable for a Princely stomach and constitution.

On the morning, when the Prince arose, Green Sleeves said, "I have a cask of lint-seed to sow which you must sow, reap, and have the seed in the cask in the same condition as that which I give out to you, before tomorrow night."

As before, Blue Wing came in, and again set her little Fairy emissaries to work—part of them cultivating the ground, part sowing the seed, part reaping, and so on, until the whole task was finished by the evening.

This being done, the Prince waited in the fields until Green Sleeves appeared; who, when he had observed that the work was finished, ordered the Prince home to his supper and bed, which was as usual, but Blue Wing continued to be his friend, and gave him a comfortable supper and bed as before.

In the morning, Green Sleeves had another task for him to perform, which, if he accomplished correctly, was to be the last. The Prince was then put to work cleaning the stable—where there had stood for two hundred years, two hundred horses—and tasked with finding, among the dung, a golden needle which had been lost by his grandmother, about a thousand years before.

The task, like all the former ones that had been imposed on him, was impossible for him to accomplish alone, but Blue Wing came again and set her little family to work—who cleaned the stable of its rubbish, found the long lost needle, and gave it to the Prince—with an injunction not to let her father know that she had assisted him in any manner, should he put such a question to him, or even insinuate as much.

The task now finished, Green Sleeves came in, and on receiving the golden needle said, "I suppose my daughter, Blue Wing, has greatly assisted you in all your tasks, or you never would have got them accomplished."

But the Prince, as desired, denied it. Blue Wing also informed the Prince that her father would offer one of his daughters to him in marriage, but to be sure to accept none of them, for if he did, they would immediately murder him.

"But as it will be somewhat difficult for you to identify us, as you will only see us through a small hole in a door," she explained, "I will tie a blue thread around my finger, and hold it out, so that you might take hold of it, and cause my father to open the door, as you want my hand in marriage; for, if you once let go of my finger, I will be lost to you forever."

All as Blue Wing foretold him came to pass, for Green Sleeves caused first one daughter and then the second daughter to pass before him; but the Prince would accept none of them until Blue Wing came, who held out her finger, which he seized and commanded the door be opened.

Her father taunted him a good deal about his foolish choice, saying, "The other two are more handsome and wise women. You have chosen the worst of the three." But being determined to stick to his agreement, the Prince retained the third daughter.

On the next morning, the wedding was to be solemnised, but Blue Wing had previously instructed the Prince not to drink any of the wine at the marriage feast, as it would be poisoned, but to have a horn prepared by their sides, into which they were to pour the wine.

This being done, Blue Wing baked three magical cakes with the wine and hung one to each of the bedposts of the bed in which they were to sleep that night, which would provide an answer to any question put to them.

The Prince and Blue Wing, instead of going to bed as anticipated by Green Sleeves, mounted two of the best horses in the stable and, with all haste, rode off.

Green Sleeves, imagining that the Prince and Blue Wing would be now asleep in bed, as he had determined to murder them, went to the bedside and asked if they were asleep.

One of the cakes replied, "We are not," and seemed very much displeased at the untimely visit.

A little while later, he went a second time, and received the same repulse, and so on a third time, when the cake in the back of the bed informed him, "Your daughter and the Prince have gone off, long ago, and are now many hundreds of miles away."

This enraged Green Sleeves greatly, and so violent was his passion that he determined to devour the old woman, as he said she was art and part in the knowledge of their flight. He then put on his seven-league boots and followed the Prince and Blue Wing with all speed.

Upon observing him coming up so fast, they were afraid that they would now be murdered, but Blue Wing said to the Prince, "Put your hand into one of the horses' ears and you will find a small piece of wood, which, on throwing over your left shoulder, will immediately turn into a great wood."

This having the desired effect, Green Sleeves had to return and call his hewers of wood to cut it down. The field was no sooner cleared of the great wood than he pursued them again with all vigour.

On his coming up behind them a second time, the Prince became fearful. But to allay his fears, his Princess desired him to put his hand into the horse's other ear, where he would find a small stone, which, when taken out and thrown over his left shoulder, as he had the piece of wood, there would arise a very great rock.

This also being done, Green Sleeves had to return a second time and call all his quarriers to cut away the rock. He then pursued as formerly; but when he was nearly upon the Prince and Princess, there being a drop of water at the horse's nose, it was thrown as the others had been, over the Prince's left shoulder, when instantly there appeared a great river.

This made Green Sleeves return a third time for all his ship-carpenters to build him a ship for him to sail across the river, and so he again mastered this difficulty, and got across the river, pursuing with all his might the fugitive Prince and Princess.

The Prince now became more fearful than ever, thinking all means and sources of escape had been exhausted, and nothing but inevitable death awaited them.

The Princess, however, informed him there was still a way left to them for deliverance, and desired that he go to the top of a high hill as fast as possible. "There you will find an egg in a certain bird's nest, which you will take out, and if you strike my father on a particular part of his breast, he will fall immediately. But if you chance to miss that spot, we are both gone."

The Prince, as good fortune still attended him, found the

egg, which had the desired effect, for he had no sooner thrown it than Green Sleeves fell, which rid them of a very troublesome enemy.

They now pursued their journey in peace, until within a few miles of his father's kingdom, when she requested him to pursue his route alone, but to inform his parents on his first arrival at the court, the good services she had performed for him, at which they would summon her with great honour and respect. But if she were to go with him immediately, they would conceive her to be some lightsome leman.

She also warned him, "Beware of allowing anyone to kiss you, for if you do, you will then think of me no more, and forget all that I have done for you."

This he determined to keep in mind, but unluckily a little lapdog in the height of his kindness kissed the Prince, which had the effect as foretold by the Princess, of making him forget his Princess, Blue Wing.

The Princess, having continued for a long time in the place where she had been left, went up into a tree near a Goldsmith's house, from which came the Housemaid with a pitcher to draw water from a well beneath the tree.

But seeing the shadow of the Princess in the water, and thinking it to be her own, she got quite vain, broke the pitcher, and said it was a shame for such a beauty to act in the capacity of a servant to such a mean man.

The Housemaid, therefore, went away to seek a better fortune, and not returning, the Housekeeper came to the well next, when being puffed up with the same vain and false delusions, went also away to another place.

The Goldsmith now wondering much at their long stay, went himself to the well, where seeing the likeness of a female in the water, suspected the cause of their disappearance, and remarked to himself, "If I had not known myself to be a man, I also would have been deceived."

So, looking up to the tree, he saw the Princess, whom he charged with being the cause of his servants absenting themselves from his service.

She replied, "I cannot help their indulging in such foolish notions, but if you will take me home to your dwelling, I will endeavour to make up for your loss by my steady perseverance in the way to please you."

The Goldsmith accordingly agreed, and home they went together. She continued in his service until it happened one day that the young Prince, her husband, was going to be married, and he sent his Groom to the Goldsmith to get ready gold mounting for the horses.

But the Groom, seeing the Princess in the capacity of a menial, was so taken with her beauty, that he made love to her, and offered her a considerable sum of money if she would consent to lie with him all that night.

This she agreed to, but upon conditions that she was to undress and go first to bed. This being done, she said she had forgotten to set down some water by her master's bedside, and needed to rise and do it.

But to prevent her from rising, the Groom went to do it, which was sooner done than she commanded him to stand still in the posture he went, and to continue that way all night.

The Groom endeavoured with all his might to set himself at liberty, but could not succeed. He then offered her all the money they had agreed upon for the bedding, to set him free, and he would never make such another proposal to her.

Upon these terms she liberated him, refusing his money, but requesting him to publish her beauty and powers wherever he went and whenever he had an opportunity, particularly before all the noblemen in the court.

As soon as he was at liberty, he did as he had promised,

when the Duke of Marlborough went to find her out, which was easily done. He, like the Groom, bargained with her for a very large sum to have the pleasure of sleeping with her that night.

However, as on the former occasion, she went first to bed, and observed to the Duke that she had forgotten to cover up the fire for fear of danger, but he agreed to do it to prevent her from rising from the bed.

He had no sooner taken the shovel in his hand to perform the work than she commanded him to work in that manner all the night, or until she released him. He soon saw he was duped, and begged her to free him from such an ignominious task, and she should have all the money agreed upon, and not be subject to lie with him as proposed.

The Princess refused the money, and set him at liberty upon conditions of his taking her as his partner to a splendid ball that was to take place at court shortly afterwards. This he promised faithfully to perform, and when the ball commenced, the Duke had one of the most handsome and beautifully dressed partners in all the hall.

After they had danced until all parties were wearied, it was proposed that they should sing a song, or tell a tale about for their future amusement. Everyone having sung a song, or told a tale, it came to the Princess' turn.

When she was reminded of her duty, instead of singing or telling a tale herself, she put down on the floor a golden cock and hen, with a few grains of barley and oats. The hen began to abuse the cock in the following manner:

"You are now like some other people in this world, you soon begin in the time of your prosperity to forget what I have done for you in the time of your adversity; how I built a house for you, sowed the lint-seed, and cleaned the stable, and found the golden needle."

These put the Prince in remembrance of everything that

had taken place regarding himself, and that the Lady was no other than his favourite Blue Wing, to whom he had formerly been married.

The Prince's other Lady was set at liberty, and the Princess, Blue Wing, reinstated, with all the honours and joys that love and gratitude could devise. They lived together happily for many years, and saw a thriving and beautiful generation rise in their place, who did honour to their education and talents.

**Aarne-Thompson-Uther [ATU] Classification of Folk Tales**
II. 300-749: Tales of Magic
   II.i. 300-399: Supernatural Adversaries
      *II.i.xii. 313: The Magic Flight*

# IX

## *The Princess with the White Petticoat*

There once was a King who had an only daughter, but her mother, the Queen, died while she was young. The King married another Queen who also had a daughter, but she was far less beautiful than the King's daughter. The new Queen was grieved at this, but more particularly when all the Princes paid their addresses to her, and no one seemed to pay heed to her favourite daughter, who was morose and ugly.

The Queen then determined to dispose of her stepdaughter by some means or another, that her own daughter might get married to one of the sovereign Princes who had been making love to the other. She then proposed to marry the King's daughter to an old doited King, a near relation of her own, that her stepdaughter might no longer be a barrier in the way of her own daughter's good fortune.

However, all her wiles and stratagems availed her nothing; nor would she listen to the voice of the old King, who used very fair and flattering words to gain her stepdaughter over to his embraces.

When fair means would not do, the Queen tried foul; and for that purpose, one day, she sent her stepdaughter to a neighbouring wood to take the air and to refresh herself, as she pretended to care a great deal for the King's daughter. But her real intention was that the old King, with a few of his accomplices, might find and carry her off when unsuspected, and when she was out of the reach of assistance from her father.

The Princess, having gone to the wood as desired, was amusing herself with collecting some of the little variegated flowers that had sprung up in her path through the wood, when a bird fluttered over her head and warned her of her danger: "Flee, flee, ever you married be!"

This timely notice caused her to leave the place immediately, and to wander where she knew not where. However, in the midst of her aberrations night came on, and with it despair, for she had now lost her way and was many miles from her father's palace.

She then sat down and cried, until—on looking wistfully around for some kind and friendly shelter—she observed at a little distance a glimmering light, which partially shone through a thicket of brambles, and for the first time, it raised in her a ray of hope.

She then directed her footsteps to where the light shone, and in a short time, found herself in a snug little cottage without any inhabitants. As she approached the fire to warm herself, she heard the noise of horses, and the voice of men coming near, which again made her uneasy.

She then thought of secreting herself in some convenient place in the house—as she was loath to venture out, and expose herself a second time to the inclemency of the weather, and the risk of being devoured by wild beasts—and so found a place, but it was not sufficiently secure, for shortly afterwards there arrived a company of gentlemen in the habits and dress of huntsmen; although, in reality, they were young Princes.

After they had caroused and eaten and drunken heartily, one of them started up as if he had heard or seen something unknown to the rest, and declared, "There is some person in the house besides ourselves."

Some of the others rose in opposition to this, and said that it could not be; but to their amazement and surprise, out came the Princess from her lurking-place, ready to die for fear, as some of them offered rudeness to her.

One of the young Neros, however, stood up in her defence, for she told them she was but a poor wanderer and designed no harm, but his strength failed him, as he had to contend with a good many, who seized her by a golden girdle she had round her body; but as it broke, she escaped, and carried with her the other half.

Having again been put to her wits' end, she at length arrived at a King's palace and asked for lodgings, which she obtained.

Next, she inquired, "Can I get a place as a servant for the family?" She was answered that she might.

On their requiring to know her name, she said, "It is Jenny White-Petticoat, and I am willing to assist in doing anything of which I am capable."

She was then put into the kitchen to assist the cook, but rose from post to post until she became one of the Maids of Honour to the young Princess.

Now, the Princess' brother had made love to several of the Ladies at court, yet none had gained his heart but Jenny, who, he was sorry, was so far below his degree in birth and parentage, not knowing her history.

The Prince communicated his feelings to his sister, and wished for her advice and assistance in making the selection of a wife for him from among the Ladies.

She then proposed to him, "Let us try an experiment which I have in mind, and which will infallibly put you upon a sure plan of knowing the best woman."

The Princess feigned sickness, and sent for one of the Ladies to come and visit her, which was no sooner done than she said in secret, "I am with child to my footman."

The Lady, by way of consolation, answered, "I also have a child to my footman, but now pass for a virgin as pure as anyone." The Lady also bade the Princess not to despair, for she would soon recover from that, and no one would know.

The Princess sent for another Lady, who told her she herself had two children, one to the footman, and another to the groom, but now was as pure a maiden as ever.

A third Lady was sent for and told the same story as the former, when she answered, "Having one child is but a trifle, for I have had three—one to the footman, one to the groom, and another to the butler, and still pass for a virgin as well as any at court."

At length, the Princess sent for Jenny White-Petticoat to whom she also told the same story as she had done to all the former Ladies, but was answered in quite a different manner.

"You are a disgrace to royalty," Jenny said, "and therefore ought to be burned. And what's more, I would assist at your execution, for it is not fitting that you should live the life of a Princess."

"Hold, hold," said the Princess, "I am innocent. It is all a trick to discover who of the Ladies of the court have been chaste, and who have not, in their early years—and I have been successful. You, I find, have been faithful, and to you alone shall my brother, the Prince, pay his addresses, if agreeable to you."

Jenny gave him permission to become her suitor, and afterwards informed him that she was the wanderer whom he had defended some time ago in the hunting lodge, when attacked by the rest of his companions. And as proof of what she asserted, she produced the other half of the broken golden girdle, which she had preserved as a memorial of the danger she had been in.

They were subsequently married, upon which she made known her whole history, which delighted the Prince greatly. Afterwards, she let her father know she was happily married, and to whom, which he received with immense joy, and following that paid them a visit. They lived long and happy.

**Aarne-Thompson-Uther [ATU] Classification of Folk Tales**
II. 300-749: Tales of Magic
    II.iv. 500-559: Supernatural Helpers
        *II.iv.ix. 510: Cinderella and Catskin*
IV. 850-999: Realistic Tales
    IV.iii. 880-899: Proofs of Fidelity and Innocence
        *IV.iii.vii. 886: The Girl Who Could Not Keep the Secret*

# X
## *The Black Cat*

In Fifeshire there once lived a farmer who had a lazy son, unwilling to do anything but enlist as a common soldier. After having taken the bounty and squandered it away, his Colonel, who was a very harsh man, ordered him abroad, where the Governor of the place treated him very ill.

Tom—for that was the soldier's name—deserted from his regiment and fled to a distant part of the country, where he met with an old woman to whom he told his tale of woe.

She advised him, "Go to the King, and lay your case before His Majesty, who will redress all the wrongs done to you."

Having done as suggested by the old woman, Tom was sent away to a castle a little distance away to sleep, where he again met with the old woman, who told him, "Speak to and tell your wants to a black cat, which will come in and follow your commands."

About the middle of the night, as the soldier sat pensive and uneasy, the black cat—as foretold by the old woman—came in. Tom said, "Come along, my bonny cat, I have long been waiting for you."

She said, "Who bade you speak?"

He told her, to which she said, "Two men will come in, but never do anything they request of you until one of a higher deportment arrives, and when I touch you, do as he bids you."

A little time later, in came three men, who said, "Rise and let us sit down."

But Tom paid no attention to them.

Another man who came in said, "Follow me."

The black cat touched Tom, so he followed the stranger, who said to him, "I was King of this castle, but was murdered by my steward, who fled abroad, and is now your Governor. Tell this to my son, the King, who will bring him to punishment, and we will never trouble the castle anymore. The three men you saw were my murderers, and they do all the mischief that lies in their power."

They then vanished, and the soldier went and told it all to the King, who gave him a letter for the Commander-in-Chief.

Tom went as directed, and arrived safely at the place, who, when he was recognised by a fellow soldier, was much pitied, as he feared Tom would have to undergo some dreadful punishment for his desertion.

Next, Tom met an Officer who gave orders to place him in close confinement and afterwards sentenced him to die; but having sent the King's letter to the Commander-in-Chief, he was soon after set at liberty.

The Governor was then secured and, with a strong guard, sent to the King, who commanded that the Governor be beheaded without judge or jury, and Tom made Governor in his place.

Tom, now having power, reduced the Officer to a Private and raised the Private to be an Officer. He then sent for his father and lived a happy life.

**Aarne-Thompson-Uther [ATU] Classification of Folk Tales**
II. 300-749: Tales of Magic
    II.i. 300-399: Supernatural Adversaries
        II.i.xxi. 326: The Youth Who Wanted to Learn What Fear Is
            *II.i.xxi. A: Soul Released From Torment*

# XI
## *The Widow's Son and an Old Man*

There was a poor widow who had many children, and to whom she could not provide sufficient meat or clothes. One night, in order to still their clamorous tongues, and to get them quietly to bed, she put a stone into the pot, making them believe at the time that it was meat, and it would be ready before they were awakened.

A little while later there came in a stranger who asked for lodgings, but as there was no meat in the house to give him, the widow told him, "You cannot lodge here tonight, as I have nothing for supper."

On seeing the pot on the fire, he asked her, "What does it contain?"

She told him, to which he then replied, "On the contrary, it contains a leg of excellent mutton which I will show you;" and taking it out of the pot, he convinced her of its reality.

The stranger next requested of her, "Please, go to the other end of the house. There you will find a chest filled with bread and other provisions."

The widow found the bread as he had said, and awakened her children to partake of it. After having eaten heartily, the eldest boy begged the stranger to tell them some amusing little tale, with which he readily complied.

The tale being told as requested, the stranger asked for payment from the boy, who replied, "I have nothing to give."

The stranger then took the boy with him to a riverside, where he threw him in and turned him into a fish, and bade him, "At the end of seven days, tell me what you can give."

But when the time had expired, he asked the boy the same question as he had done before, and received the same answer.

He then turned the boy into a serpent, which twisted itself around a large tree, and at the end of seven days, asked the former question, and received the former answer.

Next, the stranger turned the boy into a magpie, and at the end of seven days, asked the former question, but now he received a different answer: the magpie prayed heaven to bless him for so good a story.

The stranger then replied, "If you had said this at first, you would have saved yourself and me both unnecessary trouble. Go now to that old castle, which is enchanted, and kept by a Giant, not far off. The guards in it will all be fast asleep.

"After having gone through many rooms, you will find the King of Scotland's daughter sleeping on a marble table. Touch the talisman above her head, and she will awaken and teach you what is best to be done for her recovery, and those in the other apartments of the castle."

Saying this, the stranger left him.

The young man went and found everything as the stranger had told; so that when the Princess awoke, she asked him how he had gotten through the guards, which he answered, together with many other questions.

She then told him, "The Giant's life lays in an egg, which if destroyed, he will immediately die. It is kept by an old woman, who, if you can dispose of her in any manner, you will find the egg, which you can easily break, and when broken, we will be safe."

The Princess then directed him to the abode of the old witch, which he found, and bidding her a good morrow, said, "You are not well, I see."

"No," said she, "but if you would take me to the air, I would be better."

He then took her upon his back and threw her into a large fire, when she went out of the chimney with a noise resembling thunder. He next found the egg, which he also destroyed, and the Giant fell with a tremendous crash, a corpse on the ground before the castle.

Then all the prisoners who slept awoke, and testified their joy, and gave him thanks for their deliverance. Each went their own way, and he went home with King Malcolm's daughter, and received her in marriage from the old King, as a testimony of his gratitude for her deliverance.

The King also conferred on him some of the courtly honours, and it is said to be from him that the Dukes of Buccleuch have descended. They were afterwards blessed with a numerous and happy family.

**Aarne-Thompson-Uther [ATU] Classification of Folk Tales**
II. 300-749: Tales of Magic
   II.i. 300-399: Supernatural Adversaries
      *II.i.iii. 302: The Ogre's Heart in the Egg*

# XII

## *The Widow's Son and the King's Daughter*

There was once a widow who had only one son whom she indulged in every habit of laziness, never making him do any kind of work for fear of offending him. At length, her finances became exhausted and it became necessary for her to ask for some oatmeal on credit.

But having applied to a neighbour, she was refused with the sarcastic remark, "You should put your son to work for you, and then you would not be under obligations to anyone."

Having returned empty-handed, and with want staring them in the face, for the first time, she now told her son, "You must do something for a living, as I cannot support you any longer."

Jack took the hint, and next morning arose by break of day, packed up his little wardrobe, tied it on his back, and in this manner took his departure.

After having travelled the greater part of a long summer day, he stopped at a house near a wood, where he asked for lodgings for the night, as he was faint from want of meat and weary with travel. His request was granted, and some meat set before him, of which he ate greedily.

The master of the household said, "You should be working, and not going about idle."

The young man replied, "I would, most cheerfully, if anyone would employ me."

The Farmer then sent him to the field to herd cattle, but strictly enjoined him, "Do not go near that field, where a Giant lives, for if you do, you will undoubtedly be devoured, and the cattle sacrificed to the hungry maw of the greedy Giant."

Jack had not long herded the cattle, when he espied the tempting fruit that hung upon some trees in the Giant's forbidden garden; he longed to taste it, and rather than not satisfy his longing appetite, he would run the risk of his life.

Jack then went up into one of the finest trees and began to pluck and eat of the choicest of the fruit, and when an old woman chanced to pass and asked him for some of the fruit, he readily handed several to her.

In return, she gave him three black rods, with a sword, and said, "Whomever you chance to strike with this sword, they will immediately drop down dead."

Shortly after the disappearance of the old woman, one of the Giants—for there were three of them—came out and demanded of him, "By whose authority do you pluck that fruit? If you do not come down from the tree immediately, I will eat you up alive!"

The Giant's threat did not daunt the spirit of Jack, who had great faith in the magical sword; so on the Giant tearing the tree up by the root in order to throw Jack down, he was struck with the sword and laid senseless at the feet of his young master.

On the morrow, Jack went again to the orchard, and behold, another Giant came running up to him in great fury, who also demanded his business in that place; but Jack killed him also.

On the third day, Jack went to pluck the fruit, when the third Giant made his appearance and requested to know, "To whom does the cattle belong, as I must have some of them for supper?"

But Jack, who by this time had concealed himself in the hollow of a tree, cried out from his hiding place, "Ask my leave first."

On hearing this, the Giant turned round with an angry countenance, and said, "Oh, you pygmy, was it you who killed my two brothers? I shall be taking my revenge on you before long."

Jack, however, killed him as he had done the two previous Giants. He then went to their castle, which was not far off and was kept by a servant. Jack soon made this servant deliver up the keys to all the treasures in the castle, and to be at his beck and call at all times.

Jack now left this part of the country and returned home, where he found the people weeping. Having asked the cause, he was told, "A Dragon has come and imposed upon us a grave task—to give a young lady as a sacrifice to him every day, and tomorrow the Princess is to become a victim of his rage, unless anyone steps forward in her defence and rids the country of this monster."

Having heard the terms, Jack immediately ordered his man to saddle and bring to him one of the best of his horses, with the white armour. Having all things in readiness, he went to the Princess, whom he found bound to a stake, and told her the cause of his coming, that it was in her defence. "And, if you will marry me, I will save your life, or die in the attempt."

To this, she consented, and he laid his head on her knee and was lulled to sleep.

During the time he lay asleep, she wove in his hair a ringlet with white stones, very precious, and beautiful to behold. She had no sooner accomplished the charm in his hair than she saw the Dragon coming to devour her, and so awoke Jack from his pleasant slumber.

On approaching the Princess, Jack drew his sword, and stood between her and the danger to which she was exposed. He made several brave and well-aimed thrusts at the Dragon, but owing to the fire which it spewed, he never prevailed, nor could the Dragon succeed in destroying the Lady, and so was obliged to flee to save its life, for it was becoming much exhausted.

On the next day, the Dragon returned, and so did Jack, clothed in red armour, but neither was more successful than on the preceding day, for the Dragon still kept Jack at bay by spewing fire, which was likely to burn him up. However, Jack again beat it off and caused it to take wing and fly away.

On the third day, Jack chose a camel, and caused it to swallow a great quantity of water, and with it went a third time to the fight. The Dragon appeared again in quest of the Princess, but Jack, being now his match—having made the camel lie in a plentiful supply of water—dared him to the fight.

The Dragon, as on the two former occasions, began to spout fire upon Jack, but the camel in return spouted water, to quench the Dragon's fire, so that, in a little time, it was bested, when Jack laid so well about him as to deprive the Dragon of life.

Having now overcome this monster in single combat, Jack cut off its head and carried it along with him. The Princess now became his betrothed wife, when he again went in search of new adventures, until at the end of nine months the Princess bore an heir, but neither she nor her father knew to whom, for Jack had not made himself known to her nor her father previous to his going away.

The old King was now much vexed at his daughter for not knowing the father of her child, and upbraided her unmercifully as being a prostitute and a disgrace to the royal name.

This made the Princess go with her father one day to ask counsel of a Fairy, who told them that the father of the child, and none else, would be able to take the lemon from the child, which it then held in its hand.

On their return from the abode of the Fairy, the King called a meeting of all Lords, Squires, Bishops, Lairds, Farmers, and afterwards their servants, to take place at the King's palace, on a certain day which was then named, and ordered them to try to take the lemon from the child's hand—but the task baffled the power and skill of the whole multitude then assembled.

At length, Jack made his appearance, and had no sooner touched the child's hand than the lemon left it. The King then surprised, commanded that both should be put into a bottomless boat and be sent to a distant island.

They had not been long in the boat when a Lady appeared, and told them, "I am the Fairy who gave you the sword that killed the Giants and defended the Princess from the fury of the Dragon. I am still your friend." And as proof of it, she touched the boat and it became whole, and their clothes, which were ragged, became very fine.

They then returned to the harbour, dressed in all the splendour of royalty, in which they appeared at court. Great honours were then paid to them, and a rich feast prepared for their entertainment, of which they partook most readily.

After dinner, the best wine was set before them, and they were invited to drink freely, but in a short space of time, the King missed his gold cup, which only made its appearance at the table on particular occasions.

Now Jack had pocketed it for the purpose of observing the King's countenance on the discovery. The King wondered much where it could be found, when Jack said, "I thought that Kings wondered continually, for you were the same when your daughter was likely to be devoured by the Dragon."

Jack then threw down the cup, and with it the Dragon's head, saying, "Behold in me the cause of all your wonder, for it was I who stole your cup, and it was I who saved your daughter from becoming a victim to the fury of the monstrous Dragon."

And, as further proof of his statement, the Princess added, "Behold in his hair the identical ringlet which I wove with white stones the first day he attacked the Dragon."

The King then caused them to be publicly married, attended with rejoicing and feasting, which lasted many days. Jack afterwards sent for his mother and treated her with great kindness, while he inherited the crown on the old King's death.

**Aarne-Thompson-Uther [ATU] Classification of Folk Tales**
II. 300-749: Tales of Magic
   II.i. 300-399: Supernatural Adversaries
      *II.i.i. 300: The Dragon Slayer*

# XIII
## *The King of Morocco*

There once lived one of those farmers in the North of Scotland who delighted in educating their sons, and he had a favourite son who had got all the education which that part of the country could bestow, so his father thought of improving it still a little farther by travel.

Accordingly, the father and son set off together, to procure more knowledge, when they met with a stranger, who, in a familiar manner, asked, "Where are you going?"

The old Farmer told him, "I am going in search of knowledge for my son, who has taken instruction at the best schools in Scotland, but is still deficient in the principal requisites of human education."

The stranger then said, "If you would entrust him to my care, I will complete his education, and make him an expert in all that is necessary for any of the learned professions in the course of seven years."

To this the old man consented, having himself a thirst for knowledge, but asked, "At the expiry of the term, where will I find my son?"

The stranger then replied, "If you do not get him before the seven years have expired, you will not get him at all;" and where the old man was to find his son, the stranger did not let him know.

The three men then went their respective ways: the Farmer back to his farm, and his son and teacher to a place beyond the ken of humankind.

Before the end of the seven years, the Farmer began to weary for the return of his son, so went in pursuit of him.

When travelling in a solitary part of the road in an uninhabited part of the country, he met with an old man dressed in pilgrim's garb who said he knew his errand and desired him to go to Dr Brazen-nose of Cambridge. "He can inform you of your son, as it was he who gave him to the King of Morocco, where, I fear, you will have to go before you receive your son."

On arriving at Cambridge, he was told by the Doctor, "You will get your son, if you can find him."

This was all the information he received from the learned Brazen-nose; so he set off for the court of the Moroccan King, where he arrived, after having seen many strange sights, in safety.

There he asked for his son, when seven doves were set before him, and he was desired to make his choice; he did so, choosing the one with a broken wing, which chanced to be his son in the likeness of a dove.

Happy to meet again, they now took leave of the Moroccan King's court and pursued their journey homewards with all the speed they could manage.

On their way home hunger began to prey upon their vitals, but having no money by which to pay for meat, the son said, "I will turn myself into a horse, which you can sell at the first market, but be sure to be on your guard and do not let the bridle slip out of your hand, for if you do, the consequence might be fatal to me."

The old man promised, but thoughtlessly forgot the serious injunction, and let the bridle fall from his hand, which put the young man into much danger, being pursued by the King and his companions.

The young man then changed himself into an eel, which the King observed and, with six of his nobles, turned themselves into seven sharks and pursued the eel.

Being relentlessly attacked from all sides, the son next changed himself into a bird, when they did the same into eagles, and gave him chase, until he took shelter in a Lady's window, and became a ring on her finger.

When night came, he became a man, which put the Lady in great fear. He told her the danger he was in, and begged her assistance in making his escape from the King and his nobles, who were his pursuers, and were at that time at her gate as musicians, who would ask nothing of her but the ring.

"But instead of complying with their request," he said, "throw me into the fire, and I will save myself."

Accordingly, as he had said, they asked the Lady for the ring, but she threw it into the fire, which upon observing, the King and his nobles became goldsmiths in order to beat the ring.

The young man next turned himself into a sack of barley, when they became geese to eat the barley; but because of that, he immediately turned himself into a fox, and—before they became aware—devoured them all, which put an end to his troubles.

He then married the Lady and went in search of his father, who had caused him so much pain. On his travels, he happened to see a man who had two old wives whom he asked,

"What are you going to do with them?"

Upon receiving no answer, the young man said, "I could grind them together, and out of the two, produce a beautiful young one." This he did, to the astonishment of every onlooker.

Next, he made a fine young horse out of two useless old ones, which two men observing, attempted the same, but out of two produced nothing. One man also attempted to make a young woman out of two old ones, but was still more unfortunate than the former, for they only lost their horses, but he lost his wives and was condemned to death for murder.

At length, the young man put all things to right again, found his father, went back to his wife, and for many years lived happily and peaceably, much and justly esteemed by all who knew him for his great learning.

**Aarne-Thompson-Uther [ATU] Classification of Folk Tales**
II. 300-749: Tales of Magic
    II.i. 300-399: Supernatural Adversaries
        *II.i.xx. 325: The Magician and His Pupil*

## XIV
## *The Princess of the Blue Mountains*

There once lived a poor widow who had but an only son. She indulged him so much that he grew lazy, and at length would not so much as obey her in anything, so that she was forced to drive him through violence from her solitary habitation.

Having now nowhere to flee to and take shelter when the merciless storms approached, Will thought it better to take heart and pursue his fortune in a strange land.

He began his journey early one morning in May, when the trees were budded and the fields looked green, and continued until he reached the side of a rapid river, where he sat down. At times, he rose to make a desperate plunge, but, as often as not, his heart recoiled from the apparent danger he had to undergo.

During his dilemma, a Lady on the opposite banks had observed all his motions and knew his fear. She made a sign to him to venture in, which he did, and he safely reached the opposite shore.

The Lady now took him under her protection, gave him

meat and comfortable clothes, and bade him, "Be easy about your future journey."

She then requested of him to go into a beautiful garden, and pluck and bring to her the fairest flower; but after having searched it all over, he returned and said, "You are the most beautiful flower in all the garden."

On hearing this, she asked of him, "Will you accept me as your wife?"

Will most readily answered, "Yes!"

She then said, "If you knew but half of the dangers that you will encounter for me, you never would have made such a choice. However," said she, "I will do the best to preserve you. At least, I will give you such armour that, if rightly used, no one will be able to overcome you.

"Know then," added she, "that I am the Princess of the Nine Runners of the Blue Mountains, and that I was stolen away from my father's court by Grimaldin, the Demon. And it is with his legions that you will have to fight before you can set me free.

"This night you will be attacked by three legions of his Demons, but here are three black sticks, and an ointment. Each stick will beat off a legion of the Demons, and the ointment, if you chance to receive any hurt, as soon as applied, will make you whole again. Use these things well, for now I must leave you."

She had no sooner fled from his presence than the Demons made their appearance, and asked his business there, which he answered, not at all out of countenance, for he had great faith in the armour with which the Lady had chosen to invest him.

The Demons, then thinking to beat his brains out, lifted their clubs—but Will parried their blows so artfully that he received no injuries. He then fell to beating them with his black sticks, which had the desired effect of obtaining a complete victory, as the Lady had foretold.

The next morning, the Princess paid a visit to her young hero and remarked, "You are the first that has had the courage to withstand the sight of so many fierce cannibals, and I hope you will be able to encounter as many more this night."

So saying, she gave him an additional six black sticks, one for each legion, and an additional supply of the ointment, in case he was wounded.

The Lady visited him, as on the former occasion, in the morning after the second engagement, and expressed her joy at seeing him well. She told him, however, that, "Tonight, you will have twelve legions of Demons to fight, with the tyrant, Grimaldin, at their head."

Will replied, "I find myself twelve times stronger than at first, and am in no way afraid to meet with them all."

She then gave him, as before, a black stick for every legion, with more of the ointment, in case he should be, by any means, hurt, as Grimaldin was more cunning than any of the others which had come before him. She then made her departure, and Will began to prepare anew for his next encounter with the Demons.

The Demons then began to assemble in battle array, when their captain asked him, "What is your business here?"

Will told him, "I have come to rescue a Princess from your horrid enthralment and slavery, and that I will do—or die in the attempt."

"Then you shall die," said Grimaldin.

"Not yet," Will said. "I have more good to perform first."

Grimaldin then instructed his Demons to strike; but Will, having the charmed sticks, beat them all off.

Grimaldin now began to fume and rage, and made a bold stroke at Will, which brought him to the ground. But Will immediately applied the ointment, and became as whole as ever, and rose more strengthened than before, and beat off Grimaldin also.

Next morning, as she was her habit, the Lady appeared, and seeing him safe from harm, told Will, "You now have no more dangers to fear, all are past and gone, provided you will abide by my counsel."

She then gave him a book, within which was written the lives of all the Chiefs of her nation, and requested of him, "Keep reading it, and, upon no account, take your eyes off it; for, if you do, it will cause you much sorrow."

She also told him that by his due attention in reading the book, he would soon become one of her father's favourites, and be transported to the country where she was going, which was a great way off.

No sooner had Will begun to read the book than he heard many voices calling him all sorts of opprobrious and terrible names, attempting to make him look away from his book; but he withstood all their temptations.

Unluckily, however, one person called out, "Who will buy apples?" Upon hearing this, Will—being exceedingly fond of that particular fruit—chanced to gaze around him, and was immediately thrown with considerable violence against an old woman's basket.

For some time, Will knew not where he was, so much was he stunned with the suddenness of the shock. On recovering himself a little, he saw an old man resting on a seat in the shade of his cottage to whom he applied for information of the Kingdom of the Nine Runners of the Blue Mountains.

The old man said, "I do not know, but I will call an Assembly of the Fishes of the Sea, and ask it of them." He did so, but none could answer him.

He then told Will, "Perhaps my brother can assist you in

finding it, as he is five hundred years older than me, who myself am only two. But the place of his residence is four hundred miles away. However, that can be easily overcome—I shall give you a pair of swift slippers, and a ball to roll before you, which will bring you safely and shortly to the place."

The old man did as he said, and Will found himself at the second old man's door, who soon after made his appearance. Will then asked him, as he had done his brother, but he could not inform him without calling a Council of the Birds.

Shortly after having done so, they all appeared at his call, apart from one very old Eagle; but none of them knew.

At length, the Eagle arrived, who excused himself by saying that he had been long away, "As I was engaged in carrying a witch to a far distant place of the world."

The Eagle was then questioned as to his knowledge of this Kingdom, who replied, "I know it well, and have orders to carry Will on my back to it, with a good supply of oxen and other provisions."

They then mounted, and the Eagle flew off. When they arrived at the Kingdom, they alighted, and Will dismounted. He had not travelled long until he reached a house with black hung around, where Will asked for lodgings, but was refused.

He was then told, "It is on account that the proprietor of this house is this day to suffer death, having been selected for that purpose by a Giant, which has come from an unknown country, and is making our nation pay by giving him a human victim daily as a sacrifice for his table."

"And the King's daughter has been offered in marriage to anyone who will deliver our country from this terrible cannibal," added another. "She who was once delivered from the oppression of Grimaldin by a Scottish Chieftain, but lost him on her return to her father, which she regrets mightily."

Hearing these things, Will again dressed himself in

armour, went out the next morning, and—after a hard struggle—slew the Giant. He was then recognised by the Princess, who told her father, who at once consented to their union, and at his death bestowed his Kingdom on Will. Will then sent for his mother, and they lived all together, long and happy.

**Aarne-Thompson-Uther [ATU] Classification of Folk Tales**
II. 300-749: Tales of Magic
    II.ii. 400-459: Supernatural or Enchanted Wife, Husband or Other Relative
        II.ii.i. 400-424: Wife
            *II.ii.i.i. 400: The Man on a Quest for His Lost Wife*

# Notes

### THE RED ETIN
1. (p.2) **Etin** (or *Etyn*) – A British word for *Giant*, which survived longer in Scotland than England

### RASHEN COATIE
2. (p.26) **Rashen Coatie** – in the Scots Language, *rashes* equates to *rushes*, the family of marsh plants with cylindrical stems; *rashen* and *rashin* are derivatives which mean 'made from, composed or consisting of rushes;' hence the name of the Scottish Cinderella, who wore a coat of rushes, being *Rashen Coatie* (or *Rashin Coatie, Rushen Coatie, Rashie Coat* etc.)
3. (p.28) **Burn** – a brook or stream

### THE THRIFTLESS WIFE
4. (p. 38) **Clew** – a ball of thread, yarn, or twine
5. (p. 38) **Web** – a piece of woollen cloth; fabric on a loom
6. (p. 38) **Worsted** – a closely twisted yarn or thread made from combed long-staple wool
7. (p. 39) **Braw** – fine, illustrious (of things, clothes)
8. (p. 40) **Winnow** – to separate grain from chaff by fanning

## GREEN SLEEVES

9. (p. 45) ***Sloeberry*** – the sloe(berry) is the small sour blue-black fruit of the *Blackthorn*, which is a thorny European shrub with small white flowers
10. (p. 48) ***Lint-seed*** – another name for *Flaxseed*, it the seed of the *Flax* plant, which yields *Linseed Oil*
11. (p. 50) ***Art and Part*** – a term used in Scots law to denote the aiding or abetting in the perpetration of a crime
12. (p. 52) ***Lightsome Leman*** – a frivolous lover or paramour

## THE PRINCESS WITH THE WHITE PETTICOAT

13. (p. 56) ***Doited*** (or *doitit*) – {chiefly Scots} not of sound mind; impaired in intellect; foolish or childish, as from senility
14. (p. 58) ***Neros*** – Any cruel and wicked tyrant, referring to the Roman Emperor, Nero Claudius Caesar Drusus Germanicus, who ruled 54-68 CE, and became notorious for his despotism and cruelty, and was alleged to have started the fire of 64 CE that destroyed a large part of Rome

## THE BLACK CAT

15. (p. 61) ***Bounty*** – A payment or subsidy, especially when made by a government, such as an extra allowance to induce into the armed services

## About the Adapter

*Rachel Louise Lawrence is a British author who translates and adapts folk and fairy tales from original texts and puts them back into print, particularly the lesser-known British & Celtic variants.*

*Since writing her first story at the age of six, Rachel has never lost her love of writing and reading. A keen wildlife photographer and gardener, she is currently working on several writing projects.*

**Why not follow her?**

  /Rachel.Louise.Lawrence

  @RLLawrenceBP

  /RLLawrenceBP

  /RachelLouiseLawrence

Or visit her website:
**www.rachellouiselawrence.com**

# Titles Available as Audiobooks

### Ancient Scottish Tales
*Traditional, Romantic & Legendary Folk and Fairy Tales of the Highlands (Unabridged)*
Narrated by Angus Yellowlees

### Hansel and Gretel (First Edition)
*The Original Brothers Grimm Fairytale*
Narrated by Joseph Tweedale

### Nutcracker and Mouse King
*The Timeless Christmas Fairytale (Unabridged)*
Narrated by Savy Des-Etages

# Other Titles Available

### Madame de Villeneuve's
### THE STORY OF THE BEAUTY AND THE BEAST
*The Original Classic French Fairytale*

Story by Gabrielle-Suzanne Barbot de Villeneuve
Translated by James Robinson Planché
Adapted by Rachel Louise Lawrence

*Think you know the story of 'Beauty and the Beast'? Think again! This book contains the original tale by Madame de Villeneuve, first published in 1740, and although the classic elements of Beauty giving up her freedom to live with the Beast, during which time she begins to see beyond his grotesque appearance, are present, there is a wealth of rich back story to how the Prince became cursed and revelations about Beauty's parentage, which fail to appear in subsequent versions.*

**If you want to read the full story of Beauty and the Beast, look no further than this latest unabridged edition...**

ISBN-13: 978-1502992970

### CENDRILLON AND THE GLASS SLIPPER

Story by Charles Perrault
Translated by Rachel Louise Lawrence

*Her godmother, who was a fairy, said,*
*"You would like to go to the ball, is that not so?"*

When her father remarries, his daughter is mistreated and labelled a Cindermaid by her two new stepsisters. However, when the King's son announces a ball, Cendrillon finds her life forever changed by the appearance of her Fairy Godmother, who just might be able to make all her dreams come true...

**Enjoy this new translation of the most famous and beloved version of the Cinderella fairytale in all its original glory with silhouette illustrations by Arthur Rackham (1867-1939)**

ISBN-13: 978-1546510192

## SNOW WHITE

Story by Jacob and Wilhelm Grimm
Translated by Rachel Louise Lawrence

*"Mirror, mirror on the wall,
Who in this land is fairest of all?"*

The most famous of the Brothers Grimm fairy tales, *Snow White* is the story of a girl—as white as snow, as red as blood, and as black as ebony—who is the victim of a jealous Queen. But, with the help of seven dwarfs, she might just be able to live happily ever after...

**This edition includes eight colour and nine black & white illustrations by Franz Jüttner (1865-1925)**

ISBN-13: 978-1522724735

## ALADDIN AND THE WONDERFUL LAMP
*A Classic Folktale from the 'Arabian Nights'*

Story by Antoine Galland and Hanna Diyab
Translated by Richard Francis Burton and John Payne
Adapted by Rachel Louise Lawrence

*Scarce had Aladdin's mother begun to rub the Lamp when there appeared to her one of the Jinn, who said to her in a voice like thunder, "Say what you want of me. Here am I, your slave and the slave of whosoever holds the Lamp."*

One of the most famous tales of the *Arabian Nights*, the story of Aladdin tells of a poor young man who, under false pretences, is recruited by a Magician from the Maghreb to retrieve a Wonderful Lamp from within an Enchanted Treasury. Double-crossed and trapped in an underground cave, Aladdin's future looks bleak until he encounters his first Jinni, after which his life will never be the same again...

**A rich tale of deceit and magic, vengeance and love, if you want to read the complete story of Aladdin, then look no further than this unabridged edition.**

ISBN-13: 978-1092815475

Printed in Great Britain
by Amazon